THE CASE OF THE TALKING BUG

The police took a dim view of the way Harry Malone made his living. That's why they put the wiretap on his phone. And that's how they were tipped off that a girl was going to be killed at Sandy Beach.

Greg Evans, a young graduate of the FBI Police Academy, got the case as his baby. He found the girl at Sandy Beach, but he was too late. The dead girl turned out to be Jan Logan, twenty-eight, single, and as her landlady later told Greg, "a party girl . . . all washed up . . . desperate." She had lived with a younger sister, Cokie, who had left on a trip the day before Jan's death.

Then, on the Malone tap, another message: "They couldn't find her last night. She was on a trip. But it's all set up for tonight. They know where she is." *Had Jan been the wrong victim?* And Greg began his desperate race against time, to find Cokie before "they" did.

Scene: California.
A condensed version of this novel appeared in *American Magazine*.

The Gordons

The Case of the

THE GORDONS

Talking

bug

DOUBLEDAY & COMPANY, INC., GARDEN CITY, NEW YORK

M
G6.64

All of the characters in this book are fictitious
and any resemblance to actual persons, living or dead,
is purely coincidental.

(4891)

THE CASE OF THE TALKING BUG

CHAPTER 1

The call came over the police tap on the Malone telephone at 11:53 P.M.—a tap known to the Tech men as Old 66—that a girl was going to be killed. An unknown girl. It was Monday night, September 6, in the full of the moon, with the stars sparkling as they seldom sparkle over a big city.

The night had begun like many another for Greg Evans. At a few minutes after five he had brushed his way through a swarm of secretaries disgorging themselves from the Stacey Building. He was conscious of their scents, of laughter and tired faces, and occasionally a body jostling his as some girl sought to escape from the pack.

Inside the office building, he glanced back to see if he had been followed, and then walked to a phone booth and dialed.

"George," he said, "I'm coming up."

"Okay, Greg."

At the ninth floor he left the elevator, turned right, walked to the end of the corridor, and turned left. A girl came out of a door then, heading toward him, and he felt her eyes on him.

At the last office he waited until she was out of sight, and then slipped a key quickly into the lock. He stepped inside, closing the door in the same motion. He was now in what had been a secretary's reception room, but it was stripped bare. He took three steps to another door and put a different key in the lock.

As he entered, George Benson came alert out of a swivel chair, a holster bobbing awkwardly at his hip with a .38 jutting out of it.

"Hello, Greg," he said. He was the studious type who would have looked more at home behind a prof's desk than riding a police Tech.

"Anything doing?" Greg asked, nodding toward the playback machines—twenty-seven of them—that lined the room in a horseshoe arrangement. Each was a tap on a telephone—a telephone that led into homes and offices where violence already had flared or might, into the lives of killers and kidnapers and cheap hoods, as well as into the lives of innocent people who somehow or other had become enmeshed by crime.

The machines were chattering—the talking bugs, they were called.

". . . oh, you know her, Peggy, she always takes a few years off her age for good behavior . . . she's got a lot of mileage . . ."

". . . hi, Jeannie, whatcha doing?"

". . . if he talks that way to me again, I'm goin' to cut him up . . . I got a little ole butcher knife stuck under the mattress . . ."

". . . Joe, I can't make it tonight . . . I got to take the wife and kids to a show . . . Yeah . . ."

". . . what time you got, dearie, my clock's stopped . . ."

This was the busy hour. Here in the horseshoe at this time of evening they could hear all life, sweetness and gaiety, the shocking and the sordid.

Greg turned back to George. "You started to say . . ."

"We got a break this afternoon on the Number 10 bug."

Tech 10 was the phone tap on Knuckles Marston, a tough, gunmad eighteen-year-old punk who headed up the White Fence gang, a rat pack of teen-age hoodlums who had terrorized the North Side tenement district for the last five months. They had one slaying, nine knifings, and twenty-seven holdups on their record, and no convictions.

George referred to the log. "They intend to knock over Joe's Liquor Store at Fifty-seventh and East Randolph when it closes tonight."

"You taped it?"

"Yes—Miss Cabot is typing it up now. I called Robbery and Juvenile."

Greg nodded and started walking around the horseshoe, glancing briefly at the log beside each playback. He stopped at Tech 8, a tap on Mabel Sue Bend, a known girl friend of Joseph "Mugsie" Hardin, wanted for murder. The log chart read: "3:32 P.M.—Mabel to Wimpy (?)—Wimpy says someone arriving on 9:40 bus tonight—Taped."

"Who's Wimpy?" Greg asked.

"Never heard of him," George said. "I phoned it to Homicide."

Greg continued checking the logs as George sat back down in the swivel chair, which was in the middle of the horseshoe. From there he could reach any playback in one quick step and start the tape recorder beside it going if he thought the conversation pertinent to a case.

Greg stopped at Tech 12. "Anything new on Joan?"

"Her mother called. It's polio."

Greg bit his lip. Joan was five, going on six. Her mother called a friend every morning whose phone came in over Tech 12. Greg had followed Joan through the mumps, chicken pox, into kindergarten; he'd heard about the scooter Santa Claus had brought her and the puppy she'd gotten at birthday time.

George said, "Tough break." Greg nodded and walked quickly out of the room, going to a desk in a small, glassed-in cubicle. From his office he could see into the Tech Room and into another cubicle adjoining his, where Miss Cabot sat typing.

He knocked so he wouldn't frighten her. She turned, smiling.

"Is the ten tech ready?" he asked.

"I'm finishing it now."

He turned away, but her eyes stayed with him a second. She

liked the guy, the easy way he carried his tall, thin frame, the easy way he smiled and talked. . . .

When the call came through on Old 66 at 11:53 P.M., George called to him.

Old 66 had a high whine because of its age. Everyone was a tenor on it, but the Tech men kept it out of a very real affection. Old 66 had broken seventeen murder cases, thirty-three extortions, two kidnapings, and no one had counted how many rapes and aggravated assaults. The record was pasted on the wall behind it.

Old 66 was working now on the Malmo case—Malmo being a code word, a contraction of the name, MALone, with the crime, MOney. Sixty-six cut into the home phone of Harry J. Malone, a financier with offices on The Row who was a dealer in foreign commodities. He would buy wheat in Argentina and sell it in England, and copper in Chile for Hong Kong.

He had a second business that The Row knew nothing about. He was a money fence, perhaps the biggest in the United States and certainly the most elusive.

"It works this way," Greg had explained to George Benson. "Say a kidnaper gets $100,000 in ransom. He knows the police have a record of the serial numbers on the bills and he may be picked up passing them—like Bruno Hauptmann was in the Charles Lindbergh case. So he hunts up a money fence like Harry Malone who offers him $20,000 to $30,000 in honest currency. And then Malone feeds the hot $100,000 into his foreign-commodities business abroad. By the time the money filters back to the United States and is spotted, it would take a mob of accountants and detectives to trace it."

Greg had added later, "They never get enough. Look at the banker in Chicago who financed the Capone gang. He was a millionaire."

Malone himself never handled the money and never made any of the deals. A party unknown to the police, whom the telephone tap revealed only as "Hoagy," did that.

Hoagy was now saying, "Don't blame me . . ."

Malone's voice was thin and neat and almost toneless. "I want you to listen to me carefully . . ."

Greg turned away and picked up the outside phone. "This is the police department. Give me the chief operator, please."

He waited a bare second. "Lucy," he said. "Greg Evans. Will you trace the call that's on BO-82756?"

He hung up and turned back. His fingers were working hard.

Hoagy was talking. "I tell you, I can't talk them out of it, Blitz. They're going to take care of the kid."

"Where?"

"I dunno. Maybe same place—Sandy Beach."

"When?"

"I dunno much about it, Blitz. Tonight, maybe."

"Did you inform them I was furious about it?" Malone asked.

"Sure—sure I did. But they figure only two people will miss her. Her landlady and the hash house where she works."

"I thought you told me she was a college student."

"Sure—sure she is. Works tables nights."

"I don't like it."

"Me neither—but what can we do?"

They hung up then, and Greg felt his whole insides coming up. He had the phone in hand when it rang. "Yes, Lucy, I know. Thanks anyway."

Eight minutes they had to talk for a dial call to be traced through all the relays, for them to know who this Hoagy was, this Hoagy who had talked with someone, someone who was going to kill a girl at Sandy Beach.

He checked his gun, pulling it a little forward on his hip, and got into his coat, talking rapidly. "Notify Homicide. Tell Mack to ask Harbor for two radio cars. And then phone Joe Packer. Tell him I'm picking him up in five minutes."

He turned back at the door. "Be careful when you talk with Mack. Don't let him know it was a tech. Say an informant tipped us off."

CHAPTER 2

He felt the thrum of the motor picking up tempo. Soon the gay, bright signs whirling by were only hot, blurred blobs. Ahead of him a path opened up as the primitive, animal wail of the siren sounded.

It was six miles to Sandy Beach, traffic all the way, even at this hour. Twenty minutes. Perhaps fifteen if he got the breaks.

Joe Packer was waiting at the curb. He was always where he was supposed to be—in a clean, white shirt and with a tie knotted just so. He was a chunky, moon-faced, sandy-haired man not yet turned thirty, who was Greg's assistant on Malmo. Greg briefed him as the mileage finger climbed to 60 and then 70.

"How're we going to stop a killing if we don't know the girl?" Packer asked. He was dropping shells into his .38.

Greg didn't know, and that was the terrifying part about police work, when a man groped in the blackness and there was a tightness in his throat. . . .

The radio cars were parked behind a weather-battered fish shack near an aged pier on crutches. He felt the cool spray on his hot face as he stepped out of the car and looked down on Sandy Beach, a Mediterranean-like cove that curved for a mile. He noted two walking figures silhouetted so sharply in the moon's back light that he could distinguish which was the woman.

The officer hurrying toward them was Jacobsen, whom he had met at the last firearms shoot. He and his three companions worked out of Harbor.

Swiftly and tersely Greg laid out the situation, time goading him every word of the way. He saw the question in their eyes. What kind of an informant was this who knew so much and yet didn't know the identity of the girl?

He brushed by it. "If you'll take over that first lifesaver lookout, Joe, and if you'll watch from the second, Jacobsen . . ."

The low towers looked like boxes on matchsticks. With binoculars and the moon and starlight, the two could cover the beach. They couldn't prevent a sudden slaying, the crack of a pistol, but if there were a struggle, if the girl should run . . .

He instructed the other officers to take up posts among the darkened hot-dog and curio stands that lined the rickety boardwalk along the street. As they left he slipped out of his shoes and socks, removed his coat and tie and holster, stuck the revolver in his belt, rolled up his trouser legs, and ruffled up his hair. He hoped he looked like a beachcomber.

He struck off across the beach, the sand warm under his feet. He rolled a little because he was unaccustomed to the pull of sand. The night lay wordless and quiet and motionless, except for a late gull circling. The air had a brinish taste.

His eyes scanned the beach intently, as far as the thin, pale light carried. He passed a couple so locked in embrace they never looked up.

At the water line the silence was disturbed. Far out a ship's horn warned of its course, and closer in, the glistening white surf rode on muttering waves. Here the seaweed sprawled on the wet sand, like dead, forgotten bodies.

Then a girl ran out of the water, screaming. She scooped up a handful of sand and tossed it at the boy as he swam the last few feet. She tore down the beach away from Greg, the boy after her. Greg hurried. The boy grabbed the girl and pushed her on the sand. His lips were on hers when Greg passed and she was no longer trying to escape. She was laughing between kisses and protesting. "Oh, Charlie, not here. Please, Charlie."

He walked alone then for a time. He speculated about the Tech call. Malone had been firm, but then Malone was always firm. He had said he didn't like it, but was it because he sensed danger or was it "contrary to policy"? He lived by policies, by rules. "I made it a rule a long time ago . . ." he would say repeatedly to Hoagy.

Nor could Malone be fitted even remotely into an act of violence. Greg had tailed him a few times. He was a slight man with iron-gray hair and gray eyes who walked at a quick pace. He had a pleasant face that was a little smug. He was quietly tailored, lived with his mother in an apartment that was moderately expensive but done in good taste, and had a daughter in Stanford who was the only reminder of a long-ago marriage. He spent his evenings occasionally at the Union League club but more often in the eighty-dollar-a-month apartment of his girl friend, a quite tall brunette in her thirties named Ellen Marshall, who masked her face with make-up, conscious of every creeping wrinkle. Malone called her Marsh.

Greg had tailed her, too, until he knew every girdled movement —the ramrod back of a horsewoman set incongruously on the swaying base of a night-club stripper. A strange combination of the country club above, the burlesque theater below.

By now he had walked the length of the cove, up to the short, chalk bluff at the far end. He climbed the rocks until he gained elevation and stood a few minutes, reading the beach section by section. A white, wispy cloud had slid across the moon, but there was still appreciable light.

A man in bathing trunks strolled along the water's edge. He paused occasionally, as though looking for someone. Except for him, the beach appeared deserted.

Greg held his wrist watch close. It was one thirty-five.

The man perhaps saw him. He seemed to look up. He turned about in what might have been a quick decision, retracing his steps.

Greg followed him, synchronizing his pace. He had gone perhaps a hundred yards, walking as close to the water as the dry sand permitted, with the low thunder of the waves in his ears, when his glance fell downward. He stopped dead still, not certain whether he had imagined it. He waited until the ribbon of foam washed away and still saw nothing. He took a step backward to a point where the faint light, striking just right, turned the water translucent.

He flicked his flashlight on and off, holding it so Joe Packer

18

and Jacobsen could see, and waded into the water up to his knees, playing the flashlight over the body. It was floating gracefully, an arm caught and held by a rock. She was on her back with her dark hair streaming in the wash of the tide. Her brief white bathing suit stood out in contrast to her dark body.

Her face was almost covered. She wore a mask with a glass window across her eyes, and there was a thin, siphon-like tube that ran from her mouth and turned in an angle alongside her face, projecting back of her head. Long rubber flippers were attached to her feet.

Joe Packer was the first to arrive. "We're too late," Greg said.

"What the thunder?" Packer asked, bending low.

"She was a skin diver. The tube's a snorkel—for air."

"Skin diver?"

Greg nodded. "You swim along under the surface of the water, look at the ocean bed, maybe dive if you see something you want. It's become quite a sport."

CHAPTER 3

Some thirty minutes later the medical examiner arrived. He removed the body from the water and the window mask and snorkel from the face. She looked between twenty-five and thirty, old for a co-ed unless she were a graduate student. In a cursory examination the med found no evidence of a blow or a struggle. The obvious conclusion was that—if it were homicide— she had been held under the water in such fashion she had suffered no contusions.

From an all-night restaurant Greg telephoned Brad Lancaster, the assistant police chief, who was in charge of the department's criminal setup. His wife answered, as she always did, zealously protective of her husband's sleep.

Lancaster's voice came over, sharp as in the daytime. With anyone else he might have been gruff, but with "young Evans" he was only to the point. He called a conference for 3 a.m.

It was after two before Greg and Packer started back to town. As Greg drove, his thoughts strayed back to the beach. He had never become hardened to death. He was like a sensitive surgeon who, losing a patient, backtracks to recheck the diagnosis, the medical history, the actual operation.

Somewhere he might have erred, somewhere. Something lay crossways. He tried to pin-point it but couldn't.

He drove so slowly to headquarters that Packer remarked he could get there quicker walking. Packer was studying him. Packer studied everyone to know their strengths and weaknesses. He was a career man, intent and ambitious, and likable for his earnestness and zest and readiness to tackle the sweaty, stinking jobs as well as the heroic ones.

They stopped in at Homicide, tossed their dimes in the cigar box for cups of coffee, and heard Bill Akers' voice booming across the long room, calling to them. Akers looked like a big shaggy tramp dog. He had reached that age and spread when a man has to decide whether to wear his belt above or below his stomach. He had chosen the latter.

"It's no good for you," Akers said, stirring his coffee. "My stomach's always bubbling like Old Faithful."

He looked at Greg, who laughed on cue. A man who laughed with Akers was all right.

"We got four good leads," Akers said, picking up the transcript of Old 66's call that Miss Cabot had typed up and sent over. "Two from this. She was a college student and worked nights in a restaurant. And another from the med. She had an appendicitis operation a few months ago. And the fourth, she was a skin diver. The boys tell me there's a skin divers' club in town—five thousand of 'em—the Snorkel Whippers."

He picked up the breathing tube. "Works like a periscope, only you breathe through it. That way you can swim a few inches under the surface and see what's going on. Most of 'em, they tell me, hunt fish with a gun that's sort of a slingshot, actually. Got a big rubber band. But I guess she was just out window shopping."

Greg looked the snorkel over curiously. Six inches. If a skin diver went any deeper, he could stay only as long as his lungs held out.

Akers continued, "The med tells me you can get drunk from too much nitrogen—if you go too deep—and then you do crazy things. Some have died that way."

As Akers talked, Greg listened to detectives telephoning restaurant owners and university people, rousting them out of bed. Over and over he heard the description: "She was a slender girl, maybe weighed a hundred and twenty. Five feet six. Brown eyes, brown hair—one of those Italian haircuts. A small cut over the left eye. Somewhere between twenty-five and thirty."

The inter-com buzzed. Lancaster was ready. Akers pulled up his tie, poked in his shirttail, and got into his coat.

Lancaster was lighting a cheap stogie as they drifted in. He raked a kitchen match along the side of his desk and, putting it to the cigar, watched them over the flame. He was bantam size, restless, nervous, and forever driving. For twenty years everyone had been expecting him to drop dead.

Before they found seats he was talking. "We'll give this out as an accidental drowning," he said. "If Harry Malone or Hoagy knew we had advance information, they might suspect it was a phone tap—and that would wash out 66. Is that clear?"

He didn't wait for comment. "We'll have Harbor include it as a routine matter when the crime-beat men make their 6 A.M. check. Unidentified girl found drowned—that's all. We'll ask them to carry a description, and by the time the home editions hit we may have something."

He asked for details. They gave them to him cryptically and quickly, the way he wanted them. He had little use for an officer who couldn't pick out the pertinent points in a murder case and summarize them in a few words.

They discussed briefly whether the slaying might be the outgrowth of a money purchase, and hence an integral part of Malmo, or whether the killers were merely friends of Hoagy's.

Akers, who was strictly Homicide, was itching to check it out fast. "If it weren't for wrecking Malmo," he said, "we could pick up Harry Malone, sweat him, find out who Hoagy is, sweat him, and learn the identity of the killers."

The phone buzzer jarred them. Lancaster took the call with the cigar tight between his lips. "Yeah, Taylor . . . Okay . . . Okay . . . Thanks."

He hung up and looked at Greg, hesitating. He shook the ashes off his cigar stub. "The woman was already dead," he said thoughtfully, "when the call came over 66. The med says she died between 5 and 10 P.M."

Greg whispered, "Well, I'll be . . ." They were silent a moment, fitting this new fact in with the others. Greg felt better. They had not been too late, they had not muffed it. "Hoagy was very definite," he said, and trailed off. Something was wrong someplace about that call.

Lancaster broke up their thoughts. "I've got a new list here," he said brusquely. He stood up to see the desk better and locate the paper. He read them a record of the money Malone and Hoagy were believed to have bought: $100,000 from the kidnapers in the Blatt case, one dead, St. Louis; $35,000, Garner extortion, Denver; $75,000, First National holdup, two killed, Seattle; $40,000, Danielle blackmail, Omaha; $50,000, Sinclair kidnaping, baby strangled, Chicago.

He added, "If we can get the evidence on Harry Malone—catch him with the money in his hands—we may be able to crack every one of these cases. If we have to, we'll wait to wrap up this killing until we wrap up the whole Malmo deal. Any questions?"

He didn't wait for any. He said to Greg, "Evans, I want to see you." Akers and Joe Packer took the cue.

Lancaster sat down, staring at Greg, a habit that caused men to fidget. He never meant it the way it seemed. He respected Greg—had since the Watson case, a singularly brutal and involved gangland slaying. He had never praised him, because it was only what was expected of a man, but shortly afterward had placed him in charge of the Tech Room and, later, the Malmo detail.

"Guess you've heard about the grand jury?" he said.

Greg had. The grapevine had it that the grand jury was threatening to investigate wire tapping by the police.

Lancaster continued, "The D.A. hopes to talk them out of it, but you know grand juries. They can be pretty stubborn."

He blew out a circle of smoke. "What about the security on that setup, Evans? The newspapers would have a field day . . ."

Greg reassured him. Everyone on the Tech squad telephoned from the office building's lobby before taking the elevator. It took two keys to pass through the two doors. The place was monitored twenty-four hours a day and each officer armed. The windows were nailed down and boarded up. Even in the department itself only a trusted few knew the location of the Tech, and the information emanating from the taps was fed to the squads as though coming from confidential informants. The reports all read: "EV-16 reported today . . ." The EV stood for Evans and the 16 presumably for an informant he had developed.

Greg said quietly, "Let me go before the grand jury. Let's tell them what we're doing—the cases we've cracked, that kid we saved from being kidnaped . . ."

Lancaster looked up sharply. "Don't be a fool, Evans. It'd ruin us."

"I don't think so."

Lancaster smiled faintly. "You've got more guts than anyone I know—for a university man." Lancaster never let him forget he had two strikes against him: he was a graduate of the university's public administration school and the FBI police academy. Lancaster had no use for the "new type" officer. . . .

He walked the six blocks to Tech through a crisp dawn that promised another searing day. He was conscious still that something lay crossways, something he couldn't peg, no matter how much he thought about it.

The bugs were quiet, only their hum coming over. He found a note from George Benson. "Robbery called at 3:32. Advised that Knuckles Marston walked into the stake-out at the liquor store with four of the White Fence gang. Marston killed, others booked."

There was a second note from George. It read: "Re Joan—they don't expect her to live. She's in General Hospital, polio ward."

Greg sat a long time with his head in his hands. In his thoughts she was always a roly-poly little girl with golden hair. He had never seen her, of course, and never would. Her mother was Mrs. Andrews. The friend she called every morning was Mrs. Peet, a quiet, gentle woman Greg had talked with once. Her brother was a cheap killer hood, wanted for the slaying of a theater cashier. Sometime he might call his sister.

Fingering through the transcripts typed up by Miss Cabot, Greg located the eleven fifty-three conversation between Malone and Hoagy. He leaned back in the swivel chair, put his feet up on the desk, and stared at the words, conscious of the growing rumble outside as the city stirred.

" . . . They're going to take care of the kid . . . Maybe same place—Sandy Beach . . . Tonight, maybe . . ."

"I thought you told me she was a college student."

"Sure—sure she is. Works tables nights."

His fingers began to work nervously. He stubbed a foot against the wastebasket as he went to the locked file where the tapes were kept for thirty days and then destroyed.

He was all thumbs as he threaded the tape on the playback he kept on his desk and ran it a half dozen times, listening for meanings he might have missed, listening with budding excitement as Hoagy said, "Maybe same place—Sandy Beach." It sounded as if Hoagy were saying the slayers had been there before.

And what about ". . . take care of the kid"? Did anyone refer to a woman of twenty-five or better as a kid? Maybe.

Snapping off the playback, he kicked the swivel chair away from him. He saw himself briefly in the reflection of a glass partition as he passed—clothes rumpled, hair uncombed, in need of a shave.

On the street, the heat was already kicking up off the sidewalk. Threading his way briskly through the nine o'clock commuter crowd, he took a short cut through a department store. At head-quarters he located Akers in the coffee shop.

"I've got an idea," Greg said.

"So's McTamish," Akers countered. "He called me a few minutes ago. Wanted to know if Homicide was looking into the Sandy Beach death. I told him, hell, no, it was a drowning, wasn't it?"

McTamish covered the crime beat for the *News*—had for twenty-two years. Max Reed of Records, who remembered the first day he walked in, swore he still looked the same—slightly stooped, hungry-thin, with quick, amused eyes. But while he was an unknown punk then, feeling his way timidly, he had become the most praised and blasphemed newspaperman in the state. The *News* boasted he was "fearless." The department called him a "dynamiter."

Akers blew on his coffee. "If I could get my hands on the crum bum around here who's leaking to McTamish, he'd need Homicide."

"We can watch the papers," Greg said. "The next guy who gets his picture in . . ." McTamish paid off with photographs. If a detective gave McTamish a tip, the next time the detective cracked a case McTamish would run his picture. McTamish had turned the department into a sieve.

"I got an idea," Greg repeated. "All right if I run it down?"

Akers turned. "Look, you don't have to ask me. As far as I'm concerned, you're still on Homicide. You shouldn't be riding a tech, a top man like you."

He thought then to ask, "What's the hunch?"

Greg said, "I don't think the woman we found last night was the one Hoagy was talking about. I think it was another girl."

He was thinking, Maybe she hasn't been killed yet. Maybe we still will be in time.

He explained a little further, and Akers nodded. "Could be."

They fell quiet, sipping the hot coffee. Through the window beyond, Greg's gaze skimmed the city, burning brilliant in the crystal air. Somewhere out there perhaps a dozen killers brooded and planned, and a dozen people who never dreamed life was about to end violently for them went their routine way. The police could do nothing about eleven of them, not until their bodies were found and the phone rang. But the twelfth—this girl—perhaps they might.

He wondered idly what she would prove like, if she were worth it.

Nine hours had passed.

CHAPTER 4

His next-door neighbor, Cynthia, was weeding the rose garden when he pulled up before his own cottage, painted a monstrous yellow. He had painted it himself week ends, to his mother's consternation, a few months before she died.

"Hi, Greg," she called. She wandered over, with shirttail out, levis hugging her tightly. Her face was flushed by the sun.

"Hello there, Cyn," he answered.

She laughed. "Mom would have a fit if she knew I asked you— but have you an old shirt I could have? This one's about shot."

He grinned. His mother had passed his shirts along to Cyn, and sometimes they hadn't been so old.

"Yeah, I think so, Cyn. I'll take a look tonight."

He had started liking her a long time ago, at first because his mother had been fond of her. She had added a couple of years since, and he now had his own reasons.

"How's the writing coming?" he shouted back as he hurried up the steps.

"Please, Mr. Evans," she said, "we never speak of that."

She tested ball-point pens, writing the name "Johnson" four thousand times every day. She had found the job shortly after her father, an accountant, had suffered a stroke in July. Up to then she had planned on enrolling in a nurses' school in the fall. She had taken the disappointment in stride, without a word of regret.

"We'll get Dad well," she had said, "and then I'll go." But Greg knew that she knew he would never work again.

He shaved, showered, changed his clothes, and fed Mr. Adam, a Siamese cat who—he strongly suspected—swore on occasions.

As he drove away, Cyn waved him good-by with a weeder in her hand, a tall figure with hair the color of Mr. Adam's.

At the university employment office he requested the names of women students who waited tables. "Is one of our girls in trouble?" the woman asked anxiously. God, he thought, it's good to find people who are concerned about others.

"We don't know," he said.

He left with the names of only six girls, since the fall semester had not opened. They were all local students.

It was at the Varsity, a place of red-checkered tablecloths and strictly college talk, that he checked off his fourth name, Sharon Logan, a Spanish major. A thin man in need of a haircut looked at him from behind a cash register.

"Cokie?" he asked. "Funny, didn't know her name was Sharon." He shook his head. "Doesn't fit her—doesn't fit her at all."

She was on a week's vacation, he said. No, he didn't know where she'd gone. Come to think of it, she had mentioned going to a lake with a girl friend. He didn't remember which lake. Why was the police asking about her?

"Cokie's a fine girl," he said. "Wish my kid had turned out like her. Never can tell about kids, how they'll turn out."

Skipping the other two names, he drove to Cokie's address, 1458 Samaritan Avenue, two blocks from Sandy Beach. It was a better-type apartment house than he had anticipated, the $100-for-one-bedroom kind.

Inside he ran hastily over the names on the tiered bank of mailboxes, stopping at one with a card that read: "Jan Logan—Cokie Logan." He climbed deeply carpeted stairs, passing a Renoir print, to the second floor, but no one answered his knock at Apartment 207.

Back downstairs, he tapped on the manager's door. He was

about to go when a woman said, "Yes?" He saw a face that was party-hardened, and below it, a blue halter and matching shorts.

"I'm looking for Miss Cokie Logan," he said. Her glance said she knew his kind.

"Who're you?" she asked, tugging at the halter.

"I'm Evans, with the police." He saw her stiffen.

"What's she done?"

He didn't like it but he asked quietly, "Should she have done anything?"

She was still pulling at the halter. "You never know. They look sweet, but——" She broke off suddenly. He waited.

"You want to come in?" she asked.

"No, thank you."

"You might as well. I'm not doing anything."

"Where can I find Miss Logan?"

She said, "Oh well," and shrugged, and then, "She's gone—off on a trip. Don't ask me where, because she didn't say. Why don't you talk with her sister?"

"Is that Jan Logan?" She nodded, and he continued, "Where would I find her?"

"She works at the Buller Realty—but she isn't there today."

"No?"

"No. She didn't show up. They called."

Somewhat slowly he asked, "Did she have an appendicitis operation a few months ago?"

She glanced up at him, an odd look on her face. "Why, yes—how'd you know?"

Greg stood grim, hunched, hands in pocket. Old 66 had a high whine tonight.

"They couldn't find her last night, Blitz. She was on a trip somewhere. But it's all set up for tonight. They know where she is."

They were the only ones who did.

CHAPTER 5

A truck hurtled by on the ocean highway outside with a deafening roar, and the little motel dining room trembled under the vibration.

Cokie's hand, holding the letter from Jan, trembled too, and Gale, sitting across from her, noticed.

The waitress came along to ask if there would be anything else. "The fudge cake's nice today," she suggested. Gale ordered a piece and glanced at Cokie.

"She's not here at the moment," Gale told the waitress. "No use wasting food on her."

Cokie hadn't expected the letter from Jan so soon. She and Gale had left the day before, stopping the first night at this village twenty-five miles down the coast. She hadn't wanted to come on the trip. Everything inside her, at the last moment, had cried out against it. But Jan would have it no other way, spreading cream cheese sandwiches the morning they left, at 6 A.M., and making certain there was an extra clean slip. It was almost like the week before—before whatever it was that had happened to Jan.

Jan pretended nothing had happened, only that she was exhausted nervously. But there had been the night she never went to bed, and when Cokie stirred at 4 A.M., she found her standing by the living-room window with a strange, faraway look. There had been the phone ringing at all hours, and when Jan was gone and Cokie answered, the other party would hang up abruptly. And there had been Jan acting the "big sister" for the first time, peremptorily ordering her never to leave the apartment alone after dark.

"What's wrong?" Cokie had asked, and Jan's even temper had tail-spinned. "Nothing—and don't keep harping as if there was."

After that, she was frightened.

She returned now to her mangled hamburger, taking in the evening sparkle on the waters across the highway. Tomorrow they would turn their '48 vintage jalopy inland for the lake country.

"To hear Jan talk about men, you'd think they were her invention," she commented, handing the letter to Gale.

Jan had written: "Mick isn't right for you, sugar. I've tried a gillion times to tell you but, well, I'm not much good with the big-sister routine. Mick's been around, played the field. Don't let him give you the changed-man treatment. He's got a line for every girl he dates—and he's got plenty. I know. Why in heaven's name, sugar puss, when you have a whole slew of college men, do you have to pick on a tired old lover like Mick Foster? It beats me. Now toss him back in. This week end. If you don't, I'll have to make the supreme sacrifice and take him away from you myself. And don't think I couldn't do it. . . ."

Jan was a great one to underscore. Just like she talked. And then the very next day she'd be in a different mood and just as positive and final about exactly the opposite.

Gale finished the letter and discovered she had also finished her cake. She was a dark brunette who always had to stretch at physical-exam time to reach the five-foot mark.

She refolded the letter and shook her head thoughtfully. It was beyond her how Cokie, of all the Alpha girls, could ever have taken up with Mick Foster. It was that red hair that did it, she guessed. If you warned a redhead, she took it as a dare. And a redhead at nineteen with freckles and an upturned nose to boot—well, that simply did it. "Someone had to tell you," she said.

"Tell me what?" Cokie asked, taking inventory of her wallet.

"That," Gale said, tapping the letter.

"For your information, *he* told me. Besides, he's sweet and I like him." Cokie straightened up very straight and gave her red hair a rebel toss.

Nevertheless, Gale couldn't help saying, "Cokie, he's eaten Grandma and he's wearing her clothes."

She was instantly sorry and said so. Bless Cokie, she never got mad.

30

Cokie fished out the exact change for her check. "Three and a half per cent sales tax," she muttered. "They ought to make half-cent pieces. Do you realize how much that's costing us?"

After servicing the Ford they drove back to their cottage and got into swim suits. Cokie's was a little tight for her. It was Jan's, and Jan was thinner through the hips. "Wait till Mick sees you in that," Gale said.

The night was cooling fast and the water, after a few tries, proved too chilly. The sand was warm, though, and they sat hugging their knees.

"Look at that moon," Cokie said, "and most people I know waste it all their lives. I'm never going to, no matter how old I get."

"I'd rather look at that guy." A young fellow was trudging toward them, his narrow hips barely moving.

"Gale!"

"Well, I would—and don't act so shocked. I'm just being a normal, healthy American female."

When he was closer they saw he was a muscle man. "Pardon me," he said pleasantly. "Some of us fellows are doing stunts over there"—he nodded down the beach a short distance—"and we need someone your size to balance." He indicated Gale. "Would you mind?"

Gale looked at Cokie, and Cokie looked back. He did have a nice way about him. "Go ahead, muscle girl. I'll wait here for you."

She lay flat after they were gone, gazing at the stars, wondering about Jan, about Mick, about life. Now and then she sat up to glance down the beach. Once she saw Gale atop a human pyramid.

The sand was cooling and she slipped into the beach robe. Across the highway the moon was coming up, sending a shaft of sparkling light across the water, a highway of silver, she thought, with silver coaches drawn by silver horses. She lay back and stretched to her toe tips. Seven blessed days away from the restaurant. It was good to get away from things; you could see them better. Like in an art gallery.

Jan had the wrong slant, and somehow she had to make her see it. She'd heard her mother trying—and afterward Jan's visits had been much farther apart. If only Jan could have stayed in a small town, as she had—but she wouldn't.

That had been a long time ago—four years this October 17 since her mother had died, following her father by seven months. Jan had come home for the funeral and attended to the selling of the cluttered hardware store—Logan and Company, Founded 1922— that was mostly an aggregation of old debts. Jan had packed her up then and moved her into her own city apartment.

Jan had realized their differences. She had said, "Nobody'll believe us when we tell them we're sisters." But their only serious argument had come when Cokie insisted she wasn't going to take Jan's money. "I'm like Father," Jan had said. "I'll throw it away anyway." But stubbornly Cokie had jerked sodas, catalogued books in the university library, and worked as a night receptionist at a dental clinic. "You're a strange little gamin," Jan had remarked once.

She knew what people said about Jan. They never came right out and said it. They insinuated, which was even more hateful. When they did, she would walk away, her lips quivering, her throat swollen.

She hadn't thought much about it, deep down, until this last week when Jan had become almost a stranger, a stranger with bloodshot eyes who flared at the very suggestion anything was wrong. A stranger who was racked by nightmares, and then cross-examined you the next day to learn what she had said.

Cokie shut her eyes as a chill swept her body. It was unreasoning, illogical, inexplainable.

When she finally raised up on an elbow to look around, she was alone—in the dark. The moon was a faint disk covered by a white cumulus. The waves were growling, the wind was beginning to blow up a squall.

She couldn't find Gale, and her heartbeat quickened. It was silly, of course. Across the highway, the motel lights burned brightly and the trucks were still grinding downgrade in gear.

One came now, screeching, blasting, tires shrieking, motor back-firing.

CHAPTER 6

Two hours after Greg's identification of the body as that of Jan Logan, Homicide established that she was single, twenty-eight, and a dark-haired, dark-featured woman who was the type men call striking rather than beautiful. She had shared an apartment with her sister, Sharon "Cokie" Logan, for four years and had worked the last three as a saleswoman out of the William Buller Realty Company, 1547 Corinth Street. No motive for the slaying was immediately apparent. She was not pregnant, the first question Lancaster asked.

With the ident of the body, a compelling urgency lay hold of every officer, hurrying his thinking, his every move. Time itself was a potential killer.

An all-points bulletin and teletype carried Cokie Logan's description and car license number, with an "add": FYI AND CONFIDENTIAL: INFORMANT ADVISES SUBJECT IN EXTREME DANGER. REQUEST YOU HOLD IN PROTECTIVE CUSTODY WHEN LOCATED.

Detectives telephoned every lake resort within one hundred miles, and M and M mailed out photos. Officers talked with a score of acquaintances and friends and placed a "cover" at the post office on mail addressed to either Jan or Sharon "Cokie" Logan. The radio stations and newspapers carried stories that the police were seeking to notify her of the accidental drowning of her sister. Lancaster, the assistant chief, stood firm that there should be no hint of foul play.

Greg arrived in the Tech Room at 6 A.M. the next morning and sat anxiously by, waiting for Old 66 to talk. He tried reading transcripts, but his mind refused to stay put. He checked his watch frequently—6:45, 7, 7:10. Malone rose early for the opening of the big board on the Exchange and often talked with Hoagy at this hour.

At 7:23, Old 66 came alive with dial noises. As usual, Hoagy was calling Malone. Not once had Malone called Hoagy.

Greg stood tense before the playback, feeling his neck cords tightening. He called the chief telephone operator to request her to run a tracer.

"How're you feeling today, Blitz?" Hoagy asked. Blitz was the name Harry Malone had been known by in the old days when he sold worthless mining and oil stocks out of a Chicago "bucket shop" to suckers hungering for a big kill. No one else called him Blitz now. On The Row he was known as H.J.

Malone answered matter-of-factly, "Not so good. The pains have come back."

"You'd better see a doctor."

"You know me better than that."

"I've got a deal."

"How much?"

"Four hundred thousand. Can we handle it?"

There was a thoughtful pause, and finally, "When do they want to make delivery?"

"About the twenty-first."

"Is it coming from Kansas City?"

Hoagy chose his words carefully. "In a way. The men who picked the money up in Kansas City are out here now. But the deal won't be with them. It'll be with a syndicate that plans to collect it from them on the twenty-first."

Again 66 was quiet, and then, "I see. Offer them twenty-five."

"They mentioned thirty."

"Tell them twenty-five—and that's final."

"Okay—I'll let you know."

"Anything more on that other matter?"

Greg stopped breathing.

"Haven't heard anything. What time shall I call you tonight?"

"I'll be leaving at eight. Make it seven-thirty."

The clicks of the phones going down came almost simultaneously. Greg glanced at his watch. Two minutes and twenty-five seconds.

He was sweating as he left Tech, and sweating more as he hurried up the old worn steps at headquarters. A policeman ahead of him had a half drunk who protested, "I couldn't have walked that line, officer, even if I had been sober."

Two girls coming down the steps glanced his way, and the blonde's eyes stayed with him as he passed. At the top he turned briefly to watch as they disappeared down the sidewalk. He could understand how a brilliant detective like McKeen could get into the jam he had. Everywhere a detective turned, their kind waited, seeking to exchange favor for favor.

He felt the rippling floor inside tremble beneath his feet and its old joints groan. Max Reed of Records stopped to tell him he had found an 1880 "blotter" with the arrest booking of Big Jim Cannister, the Capone of his day. Greg promised he would drop by to see it.

The cigar smoke lay curled over Lancaster's office. He flicked off the inter-com, finished dictating a report, and looked up. Give the man three hours of sleep and he was an eighteen-year-old.

"Morning, Evans," he said cordially. "What is it?"

"Do you remember a Federal Reserve job in Kansas City? They got around $400,000."

"August twenty-eighth. Killed one officer, wounded another. What about it?"

"I think we got something on it. Hoagy asked Malone if he could handle $400,000 around the twenty-first. Malone wanted to know if it was coming from Kansas City."

Lancaster flicked the inter-com. "Don't put anyone through," he said.

Greg referred to his notes. "Hoagy said the men who pulled the job in Kansas City were out here now, and then he said, 'But the deal won't be with them.' He said—and these are his exact words —'It'll be with a syndicate that plans to collect it from them.'"

"A highjacking, huh?" Lancaster was on his feet. "And Malone's dickering with the highjackers. What else?"

35

"Nothing, except Malone is offering them twenty-five cents on the dollar. They want thirty."

Lancaster thought out loud. "The mob that's planning to heist the money must have an inside man—to know the Kansas City crowd's going to hold it that long."

"It looks like it."

"The twenty-first—that gives us a little time. If we can tie Malone in definitely on this deal, with evidence that will hold up in court . . ."

Greg nodded. Lancaster talked in tommy-gun bursts the next few minutes. He had a mind that could shake up the facts, sort them out, study them, and base a decision on them, all within minutes.

"What about the tail job on Malone?" he asked.

"It's washed out. Nothing in fourteen days. We might as well pull it."

"Okay, pull it."

"We're working the girl friend, Ellen Marshall," Greg said, and added, "She's no cheap hood."

Greg continued, "About this girl Cokie——"

Lancaster interrupted. "I know what you're thinking. We're going to let a nineteen-year-old kid get killed—to save the Malmo case."

His sharp eyes held to Greg. "Don't think I don't know what it means. I've got one myself—turned seventeen."

He shook his head. "It's a calculated risk we've got to run. Everything in police work is. You know that, Evans."

It was the old military strategy of sacrificing two hundred men to save a division. Every time an officer made a decision, whether he knew it or not, he jeopardized someone's life or welfare.

Lancaster picked up a report from the desk. "Here's a summary of the work Homicide's done on Jan Logan. I've underlined three names. Run a tap on them for a few days—see what we get. One more thing—talk with the three, so that when they come over the Tech you'll know 'em."

On his way out, Greg stopped in at Ident to phone Tech. "The big news here," George Benson said, "is that you purl one, knit two . . ."

He met Joe Packer, his assistant on Malmo, coming up the steps outside. "We might as well drop the tail on Ellen Marshall," he said. "It's not producing."

Greg thought they should keep the surveillance running another day or two, until Lancaster himself balked. "Marsh," as Malone called her, owned a small gift shop at 1854 Southport, the kind where the neighbors paid their light and phone bills. She gravitated between there and her apartment and a drugstore where she had a salad each noon.

"I'll see you at the Homicide briefing," Packer said, leaving, and Greg nodded.

He bought a paper from Paco, whose smile alone was worth the dime, the kind of smile reserved for heroes. He turned the pages quickly and found the story, a two-inch one, buried on page six. The police were seeking Sharon "Cokie" Logan, nineteen, university student. They wanted to notify her of the death by drowning of her sister, Jan Logan, twenty-eight, realtor.

Even if she read the paper, she might easily pass over the story, and it was assuming quite a bit, he thought, to think she would read the paper. He and a lot of other people he knew left the world behind on a vacation.

In the car, he scanned the summary. He noted the three names underlined: William Buller, realtor; Panther Wilson, wrestler; and Dr. C. Oxford Jones, scientist. The report listed Buller as Jan Logan's employer, and Wilson and Dr. Jones as friends. Others, too, were mentioned—and, significantly, they were all men—including Ed Anderson, a used-car dealer, and Mick Foster, twenty-six, a one-time boy friend of Jan Logan, described as the current boy friend of Cokie Logan. Foster was reported working in a logging camp, his exact whereabouts unknown, but was expected to return shortly to complete his senior studies at the university. His record showed his college career had been interrupted by five years of service in the Army.

Taking Shore Avenue, Greg gunned the car on the straight

stretches, swept up in the exhilaration that comes with movement and power, the quick pickup, the smooth throb of a motor. The old restlessness lay hold of him—the odd sensation that coursed through his blood when some deep compulsion drove him. He had to find Cokie Logan, had to find her in spite of Lancaster, and the Tech, and police strategy, and the Malmo case.

He had no trouble in spotting the Buller realty office. It was an assemblage of glass and flying beams set off from the surrounding structures by a tiny, well-manicured lawn. Buller was a tall blond around forty. His flesh looked tanned and hard as saddle leather. There was a flat place where his stomach should have been.

"Sit down, sit down," he said heartily. "I almost became a detective myself once. Could have gone with the D.A. when I came out of Princeton—but I wanted to make a million fast.

"I'm still working at it," he added with a deprecatory laugh which managed to imply that so far he had been able to make only nine hundred thousand.

Greg sat in an expensive red leather chair. "We're trying to locate Jan Logan's sister——"

Buller's cordiality changed to deep concern. "Lord, what a thing. I still can't believe it." He gave a great body shake to pull himself back to reality. "There's a sweet kid, that Cokie. No, like I told the officer yesterday, I haven't the slightest idea where she could be."

Greg nodded. "We have a report that she went to a lake resort. I thought you might have heard Miss Logan—Jan, I mean—talk about one, or know of her going to one."

Buller missed the tray in flicking the ashes from his cigarette. "Been sitting on too many escrows lately," he explained. He thought for a moment. "No—no, I don't remember. But you know how it is—you talk about so many things and they don't mean a damn until something terrible like this happens."

He absently brushed at the spilled ashes. Greg totted up the realtor's black shirt, black tie with tiny pink sea horses, and gray sport coat.

"Sure beat me up when I heard about it. Brother, did she light this place up." He nodded toward the outer office. "Look out there, will you? Looks like I'm running a home for elderly ladies, doesn't it? They've raised their kids, don't know what to do with themselves, and so what? Everyone thinks he's a realtor."

He took a nervous puff on the cigarette. "She was damn good. Handled our apartment houses. Didn't make any difference who came in, she knew what line to take. Old men, young men, old bags—she could soften 'em up."

He gave his head a short sidewise jerk. "She drove hard. Ambitious—but I like them that way. I wouldn't have traded her for that entire Egyptian mummy-works out there."

Greg nodded. "In these drownings we have to take into consideration the suicide angle."

Buller shook his head. "It doesn't figure. She didn't need money, if that's what's on your mind. She had a good take here. Only last week she wrapped up a clean little four units on Manning. Panther Wilson bought them. The wrestler, you know."

As Greg rose to go Buller said with just a touch of gravel in his voice, "They don't come any finer than Jan Logan. I'd hate to be the one to break it to little Cokie. When you find her," he added, "tell her I'm holding a check of Jan's for her—$480. The kid'll probably need it."

At the door Greg remarked casually that he understood the Logan sisters were skin divers. Buller said, "Yeah, that's right," but offered no comment.

Back in the car, Greg referred to the summary. Buller had no criminal record. His credit was double zero. He had filed twice for bankruptcy. . . .

When he neared the apartment house, he caught the flash of a plane with a red belly coming out of the sunset. In another hour Cyn would be going bowling, and he had a poignant longing to be with her, to watch her boyish figure bend low as she swung the ball expertly down the alley, to see the pleased smile as she turned back toward him.

He looked first into the Logan mailbox and saw there was nothing. Next he knocked on the manager's apartment and was waiting when he heard a door open across the way. A man stood there watching, a smirk on his face. "If you're looking for Julia," he said tartly, "she's at Mac's." He indicated the direction with his thumb.

Mac's turned out to be a sleek spit-and-polished tavern with an old film running on a television set high above the customers' heads, and someone pinking a piano halfheartedly, not in the least disconcerted by the movie's pistol shots. Everyone was too snuggled about a glass to look his way, except Julia Bunker, who sat alone in a plushy booth.

"Mind if I buy you a drink?" he asked, dropping into the seat opposite her.

"I do—unless you sit here." He moved to her side. She was in a black sheath cocktail dress that contrasted sharply with her chalky skin. Her perfume and bath powder lay heavy about her.

He motioned to the bartender. "We're still looking for Cokie," he said to her. She moved closer.

"Cokie'll take care of herself," she murmured over the rim of a cocktail glass.

"Did you hear anything today?"

She shook her head slowly in a silly fashion. "The way you fellows are hunting her, you'd think somebody got murdered."

He laughed a little.

"Cokie's all right," she said. She was toying with the olive on the toothpick. "Poor little olive," she said sadly.

"Wasn't Jan?" he asked.

"Wasn't Jan what?"

"Wasn't Jan all right?"

"Poor little olive," she repeated, and ran the toothpick all the way through. "I had to do that—to put him out of his misery."

He felt a tremble run through her.

"You want to know about Jan? All right, I'll tell you about Jan. She was a party girl. Do you know what a party girl is?"

She looked teasingly at him. "I'll tell you. She's a lot of fun when she's twenty-one. Everybody says so. All the men say so. But do you know what happens when she gets to be twenty-six?"

He could scarcely hear. The piano player had launched into "Fingal's Cave," and simultaneously the movie reached an ear-splitting crescendo of horses' hoofs.

"She's all washed up. She's lived her life. Crammed everything into it. I'll tell you something else. She's desperate. She wants a husband and nobody's interested. Nobody. I know. I was a party girl."

She was crying a little. "You're nice. I think I'll put you under my arm and take you home."

"I want to ask you something," Greg said.

"You want to marry me?"

"Did Jan go swimming much at Sandy Beach?"

"You don't want to marry me?"

"Not tonight. How about Jan?"

"I'll tell you something—even if you don't want to marry me. She went swimming. Yes, she went swimming. She'd come home from work sometimes, pop into a swim suit, and walk down to the beach."

"In her swim suit?"

"Well, what else?"

That, then, would explain why they had failed to find her clothes. Usually at Sandy Beach the women changed in the bath-houses or came with dirndls and blouses over their bathing suits and dropped them on the sand.

She slipped her arm through his as he started to go, and held on with fierce possessiveness. He was conscious of the hardness of her muscle against his. . . .

CHAPTER 7

He was five minutes late to the Homicide meeting. Lancaster was fidgeting by the door. He said nothing; his eyes said it for him.

A score of detectives sprawled in what chairs there were, while others leaned against the walls or half sat on the deep window ledges. The room itself was as sorry-looking as a vagrant. Its floor was splintering and its ceiling had lost much of its plaster.

Lancaster had called the meeting to brief the men on the Malmo case. All movement and talk ceased, as though on order, when Lancaster walked before them to introduce Greg as the head of the specially created Malmo detail and Joe Packer as his assistant.

Greg's voice was tight as he began: "Our principal subject, Harry Malone, conducts a foreign-commodities business at 128 Bridge Street. He has a good rating with Dun and Bradstreet and an excellent reputation for honesty and integrity. We'll show you movies shortly so you'll know what he looks like."

He paused as the wail of a siren came over, and then continued, "We figure Harry Malone handles between thirty and forty percent of the hot money in the United States. We're convinced from what our informants tell us"—he meant the Tech and most of the men suspected it—"that Malone never touches the money himself. He has worked out what looks like the perfect crime. His front man, whom we know only as Hoagy, makes the deals, handles the money, and disposes of it."

Lancaster interrupted. "Excuse me, Evans. I want to say here that when and if we do identify Hoagy we have no intention of picking him up—not until we have evidence on Malone. You can see why. Malone would merely recruit another front man. Is that clear?"

He turned back to Greg. "All right, Evans."

Greg continued, "We know that the kidnapers and extortionists and blackmailers make arrangements in advance with Hoagy to handle the money. I might mention in passing that in most of these cases, such as the Brinks robbery, the criminal arranges ahead of time to get rid of the money. He wants to move it fast so he won't have it on him if he gets caught."

He walked to a blackboard that ran across one end of the wall, like in an old-fashioned schoolroom. He began at the far left, working to the right.

"Now here in St. Louis—in the Blatt case," he said, pointing to a chart already chalked on the board, "you'll recall that the kidnapers got $100,000 in ransom and then bludgeoned the child to death. We know that Hoagy bought this ransom—and paid $20,000 in clear money for it. He acted, of course, solely as a fence and had nothing to do with the crime itself.

"Now our informant tells us that Malone put up the $20,000. Hoagy himself then, or a courier, delivered $40,000 of the hot money to a brokerage house in Mexico City."

He drew a line to Mexico City. "We don't know what became of the other $60,000, and I'll tell you in a minute how we know about the $40,000.

"The brokerage house was a blind. It had been set up by a confederate to handle only this one fast operation. Now, amazingly enough, Malone openly placed an order with the Mexico City brokerage house to buy $40,000 worth of rice for him in Brazil. Malone sent the Mexican brokers a bank draft for $40,000—but of course they returned the sum to him somehow since they already had the $40,000 in hot money. His bank draft was only for the records.

"Now—the Mexican brokers sent a courier with the hot $40,000 to Rio de Janeiro and paid in cash for the rice. The rice now belonged to Malone—if you're still following."

A chuckle went up at this, and everyone felt better that the tension had broken. Even Lancaster smiled.

Greg continued, "Malone sold the rice in the Philippines through a Manila broker, who remitted the purchase money directly to him."

Someone in the back of the room interrupted. "But since Malone used his own name——"

"No—Malone is in the clear. If we were to question him, he would admit he placed the order with Mexico City, just as he places orders with brokers all over the world. He would produce the bank draft to prove he paid with honest money."

Greg left the blackboard. "We know about the $40,000 because the money eventually showed up at the Chase National Bank in

New York and a sharp-eyed teller spotted it. It was traced back to Rio and hence to Mexico City, where the Mexican authorities found the brokerage house had gone out of business.

"I said this was a simple case—and it is. We have another, starting in Hong Kong, in which Malone used seventeen brokerage houses. Sixteen were legitimate."

By now the room was beginning to have an ash-tray odor and a few feet were shuffling. A murder was something you could get your hands around, but not this. Everyone had the same thought: How can you gather evidence that will stand up in court?

Someone suggested that if they could identify Hoagy and arrest him, he might name Malone.

"It would be only a criminal's word," Greg answered, "against that of a financier of high standing on The Row."

George Benson was "policing up" the Tech Room as he came in. Greg noted one call recorded on Old 66's log. George said, "It was nothing. Hoagy's calling back around eleven."

Two women began chattering on Tech 11. "When she stepped on that arachnid," said one, "I screamed."

"Stepped on what?"

"We don't call them spiders any more. Not since we read that book about what nice little creatures they are."

George groaned as they talked away. "I'm getting to be a psycho-ceramic sitting around here."

He reported that Joan, the little polio victim, had been placed in an iron lung. "The doctor says she's got a fighting chance."

Greg felt better. If that kid could only pull through . . .

As he turned away, George said, "I've been reading an article here—about the electronic menace."

He handed the magazine to Greg, who skimmed it quickly: " . . . wiretapping constitutes one more step in the creeping invasion of privacy . . . Justice Owen Roberts held in 1937 that such 'methods [are] inconsistent with ethical standards and destructive of personal liberty' . . . Many are wondering if the danger from peace officers in wiretapping hasn't become greater than the danger from criminals."

"It says our bugs are monsters," George continued. "Some of it's farfetched, but still . . ."

Greg handed the magazine back. "I know how you feel."

"You do?" George was surprised.

Greg smiled. "We're a couple of fine ones to be on Tech." George laughed.

As Greg sat down at his desk to run through the transcripts typed up for the day, he found himself disturbed. The electronic menace—wiretapping, the development of a portable television "eye" that would watch you in your home, the one-way window that he himself would help set up to "look in" on Malone's girl friend, Ellen Marshall—these and other technological developments had become a standard part of police work everywhere.

" . . . destructive of personal liberty," Justice Roberts had written.

Lancaster would say Greg was a fool, that that was what might be expected of a university man. And maybe he was. Night after night he sat here, he heard the bugs talking, he watched as they captured those who lived by violence. Sure it was an invasion of privacy, listening in on a telephone conversation, but could any decent person really care, if it meant the trapping of a kidnaper who had strangled a little girl, or an extortionist who had carried out his threat? Wasn't the saving of a life worth an occasional intrusion by the "electronic menace"?

Still, he was bothered—bothered by the burglar atmosphere of the Tech Room, the locked doors, the boarded-up windows, the constant fear McTamish or another reporter would discover the hide-out, the concealment even within the department itself, as though they were engaging in a nefarious undertaking.

He shook the thoughts off. As he picked up a stack of papers he noted the red SPECIAL sticker on a transcript of Tech 19, a tap which had been cut in only a couple of hours before on William Buller, the realtor who had employed Jan Logan. There was a notation: "See page five."

As he scanned the page, the words leaped out, and his eyes switched back to the beginning of a conversation, to re-read with more care.

Tape 267—Tech 19—4:57 P.M.

(Woman's voice.) "Hello."

(Man's voice.) "Hello, Clarissa. How's my glamour girl?"

"Oh, Bill!"

"Rudy there, honey?"

" . . . Rudy, Bill Buller wants you. . . . He's coming, Bill."

(Pause.) "Hello, Bill. How are you?"

"Fine, fine. How about yourself?"

"Oh—even six."

"Did you see the papers?"

"Un-huh."

"They've been around asking questions."

"Un-huh."

"I don't think they believe she drowned."

"What do they think about suicide?"

"I don't know. When they find out she was a no-good little witch—I don't know . . ."

"Oh, she was a nice bit of fluff, Bill."

"That's because you only drank with her. You don't know some of the deals she pulled here."

"Well, she was young—in a hurry. Look, what about lunch to-morrow? Same place."

"Okay."

End Tape 267.

Greg sat numb for a moment, the shock impact having caught him unaware. He heard Bill Buller saying to him, "They don't come any finer than Jan Logan."

What they told a detective, and what they thought . . . If you were alive, people told everything they knew about you. But dead they entered into a conspiracy, as if their silence would keep the facts from St. Peter.

A few minutes before eleven he sauntered into the Tech Room.

46

Only a cricket-like hum came over. The bugs chattered by spells. About this hour they quieted down for the night not to awaken fully until around nine o'clock. They would gossip then sporadically until noon, and take a siesta until about four, and really become a bedlam when school was over.

The dialing began at 11:08 P.M. with Hoagy running off the numbers rapidly. Greg theorized he could tell something about a man from the way he dialed. He pictured Hoagy as a busy, nervous individual, loath to analyze a situation if he could act on it.

Malone answered promptly with a thin hello.

"I set the deal tonight," Hoagy said. "At twenty-five." They heard the muffled honk of a car and other subdued street noises in the background, as though he were phoning from a pay booth.

"What about the delivery date?"

"The same—the twenty-first—around midnight. They're picking it up the same night. Zump thinks it will be around eleven. He doesn't figure on any trouble."

"What was that name?"

"Zump. You know him, Blitz. He was in the Barstow deal back in Chicago."

The line was quiet a second. "I do recall the name, but I can't match it with a face. It doesn't matter. What about the other?"

Hoagy hesitated. "Nothing yet," he said finally.

"I have a premonition about this. I don't know why—but I'm psychic. You know that. You will remember——"

"Sure, sure, Blitz, I remember. But it's the gas chamber for them if they're caught. How can I outtalk the gas chamber?"

There was another long break. "I see. Well, what is delaying them?"

"It's not so easy. They want it to look like an accident—or suicide. There's a girl with her and they haven't been able to get her alone."

"Listen."

"Yes, Blitz."

"I insist you stay out of this. Do you understand that, Hoagy?"

"Sure, sure, Blitz. Don't you worry a minute. I wouldn't ruin a setup by sticking my nose into a cheap two-bit killing. . . . How's your mother?"

"If she felt any better she'd be a juvenile delinquent."

"And Marsh—how's she?"

"She's spreading a little, thank you, but otherwise she's all right." Hoagy laughed. "It's time she spread."

Malone said hastily, "You'll phone me—soon as you hear anything?"

"Sure, Blitz, sure." The receivers went down.

As George entered the call on the log, he asked, "Who's Marsh?"

"She's his girl friend—from the bucket-shop days. Woman name of Ellen Marshall. Used to be his steno."

He placed a call to Homicide and learned the day had ended negatively. They had no more idea where Cokie Logan was, or why Jan Logan had been slain, than at the start.

If they could only put tail jobs on everyone, he thought, but the department, as a result of low salaries, had dropped to eighty per cent of its strength. Even if all the vacancies could be filled tomorrow, it still would be undermanned for a city of two million.

He was too stirred up to concentrate. He could only think of a girl like Cynthia taking long strokes through the water, or paddling idly in some cool inlet, or climbing through a green forest into the sky, a girl unaware that the moment she wandered off alone she put life behind her.

When he arrived home around midnight, Cynthia was sitting on his doorstep, still in her green bowling slacks and tailored yellow shirt. He felt the gladness rise in him as he left the car. She was someone to talk to since his mother died—someone to keep him from growing hard and cynical, which were the creeping diseases of his trade, eating the insides of a man so slowly he never knew, until one day he was forty and ill with distrust and suspicion. She would sit quietly on the doorstep, the street light glinting in her eyes, listening as he talked out the day, and then would say something that magically would still his grinding thoughts.

48

She rose as he came up the walk. "You and Mr. Adam keep the most suspicious hours," she said.

Mr. Adam heard and came around the corner, muttering.

CHAPTER 8

The stars were bright in the sky over the lake, but here under the thick canopy of pines he was only a dark, unrecognizable shape, barely discernible as a man. Even his steps as he moved restlessly about were little more than the brush of a blue jay on the soft, spongy mat of pine needles.

He could see the two girls sitting by a window in the lodge's dining room, silhouetted by the back light. He could have heard what they were discussing if he had walked into the shaft of light that fell weakly through the window. He thought about it some but stayed where he was.

He clenched a fist as his thoughts hammered at him. He asked himself why he was here and how he had gotten into this spot. He was like a common hood, standing here in the night's blackness, stalking a girl. It was the breaks, confound it, the damn, silly breaks. When they went against you, you never could tell what they might wash you into. He wanted a cigarette in the worst way. He was hungry and fagged out.

His anger swung in Cokie's direction. She was responsible somehow for his being in this predicament, and blast her, was she going to stick like a leech forever to that other girl?

It had seemed so simple two days ago. He hadn't even lain awake to think it out. It would be that easy. It would look like an accident, the same as with Jan. Only now it wasn't easy at all, because there was that other girl. There was always something. People died every day because of accidents, but when a man tried to plan one, there was one complication after another. Not until now had he realized how simple it was to use a gun or an instrument.

They left the table and disappeared. He walked a few feet to bring the cash register into view. They were out of sight again until they left by the front entrance and walked down the old board steps that groaned with age. They hesitated once, debating about something. A spotlight hidden in the shrubs flooded them. Both were in levis with their shirts hanging out. Cokie had a way of tossing her head back, and her hair, cut a little above the shoulder, would flounce like a horse's mane. She had a nice figure, he thought, and then reminded himself he had no business noticing. Little things like that could disturb the work at hand.

He waited while they crossed the road in the direction of the pier. He lost them in the darkness completely, but still he waited, until they wandered out on the pier, lighted with a string of bobbing bulbs. He struck off across the road, and at the water's edge found a log to sit on. He watched as they walked the length of the spindle-stick runway. It was quiet out there, and deserted, with the newly painted boats rising and falling with ballet grace. Even out on the lake there was quiet, not even the put-put of an outboard to disturb the night.

If the other girl wasn't along, he might this very moment be walking along the pier. He would fall casually into conversation with Cokie, and after a little blow on the head—not much, because it should look like she had fallen into the water and struck her head in the fall—he would push her unconscious form into the lake.

Thinking it over, though, that might look too similar to the way he had disposed of Jan. No, it would be better if she were swimming alone, in a quiet inlet, and he bore down on her in a motorboat. Only last week that had happened at Lake Susan. The helmsman hadn't seen the girl. The motorboat had clubbed her to death and the spinning undergear had amputated a leg.

That would be more like it. It would have the advantage of being uncomplicated and easy to execute. It would have to be in the evening, of course, when he might slip away with a motorboat. It did have a lot of "if's"—if she was alone, if it was dusk, if he was around. He couldn't stay about in the daytime. Someone might remember his face. And he should be in his familiar haunts, too, so that if there ever was the slightest suspicion people would say they had seen him.

They were sitting at the far end, their legs dangling over. He was calmer now, remembering how smoothly it had gone with Jan. He hadn't known really that he could be so clever. If he could only talk about it, tell others how brilliantly he had brought off the whole event . . .

Looking back, he thought the inspiration had stemmed from an idle remark of hers a long time ago. She had said she often went to the beach to think problems out. He had had to wait three evenings parked near her apartment house, to follow her down to the ocean. He had lain then in the sand, lost in the messy, shifting crowds, watching her. Almost an hour passed before she finally got up and headed for the rocks. He couldn't have planned it neater. It was getting toward dusk—around eight—and the other skin divers had all left and the place was almost deserted. When she donned goggles and snorkel, he took to the water.

As he neared the rocks he submerged, surfacing only for air and to take sight. He was upon her before he knew it. Her head was a few inches under water, and she was searching the ocean floor. Behind her, he filled his lungs to the bursting point, then dived. He grabbed both her ankles and dragged her down. She flailed wildly about. He had never known a woman could have so much strength in her legs. A time or two, when he had come up for air, he had almost lost his grip. When the legs no longer lurched, he had pulled her back toward the shore, unable to bear the thought of a shark devouring her. He had left her then where the water line barely covered her, and followed the curve of the beach, walking in the water so his footprints would be washed out. He finally came to the boardwalk.

If he was that clever with Jan, he would be with her sister. It was a matter of timing—and waiting—more than it had been with Jan.

CHAPTER 9

Greg rose early the next morning. He lay thinking, watching the grayness of pre-dawn filter through the window. If he ever found time, he'd have to do something about the room. He would thin out the stacks of records on the shelves that lined one wall. He would keep Glenn Miller and Benny Goodman. And the Jap flag that hung limp in one corner—he had wanted to burn it long ago because he had taken it from a dead Jap who might have had a wife, maybe even kids, at least a sweetheart. He hadn't liked the flag the day he picked it up, but it had seemed the thing to do. He would keep the silver basketball they'd given him when he had tipped in the winning shot at the regional tournament, but the college books spilled over the chest could be hidden somewhere, all except perhaps Tennyson with the lines he liked from *Ulysses.* . . . *'tis not too late to seek a newer world . . . to sail beyond the sunset, and the baths of all the western stars . . . to strive, to seek, to find, and not to yield.*

He dressed slowly, worried about Mr. Adam, who hadn't come in last night. He noted then a buttonhole was fraying and wondered if Cyn knew anything about buttonholes. After that he patted a pocket to see if he had his badge, checked to see if he was zippered up, shaved and put the toast on.

In his office at Tech, he studied the summary report from Homicide again, which listed the names of nineteen individuals who had been a part of Jan Logan's life. He picked up the phone and dialed each.

"This is a reporter on the *Mirror*," he said. "We're getting comments from civic leaders and businessmen on the China question and would like to have quotes from you."

He had no interest, of course, in their opinions. He wanted a sound track of their voices. He would break in occasionally to ask questions as they talked, and all the time the running tapes recorded the conversations.

Their voices intrigued him. He sat quiet and tense, concentrating with his eyes closed and attempting to put the meaning of the words they said out of mind. He heard only the sound, as one might who spoke another language. Panther Wilson, the wrestler Jan Logan had known, was accustomed to interviews and spoke glibly. Dr. C. Oxford Jones, the scientist she had dated, proved hesitant as he thought each word out, but even with his pauses his voice had a musical cadence and a feminine softness. The insurance man, Dan Ralston, who lived in the same apartment building Jan had, talked with great rapidity. And Ed Anderson, the used-car dealer named in the summary as a friend Jan Logan had met in a hotel bar, spit words out without bothering to modulate them.

He failed to identify any of the voices as Hoagy's. One could be, of course, because a voice coming directly over a phone would have a different timbre from the same voice emanating from a playback, especially Old 66 with its high whine.

He was interrupted once by an incoming call. "We've got the O.W. in," said Joe Packer, his assistant on Malmo. "How about taking a look?"

"I've got to stop in at Crime Lab first," Greg told him.

The O.W. was a one-way glass that would permit them to look into the apartment of Ellen Marshall, Malone's girl friend, from an adjoining apartment, without her knowing it. They had removed a large rectangular mirror over her fireplace while she was gone and substituted the O.W. On her side it would still look like the same old mirror, but on theirs, in the next apartment, it was a glass window. Slowly they were closing in on Harry Malone, to learn every word he said, everything he did. First there had been the Tech, and then loose surveillance jobs, and now the one-way mirror.

As he passed through the Tech Room, only a murmur came over, except for one bug: ". . . well, I tell you, weight just sneaks

53

up on you. One day you slip into a skirt and you suddenly notice the business behind . . ."

George Benson was sprawled in the swivel chair. "Honest, sometimes I feel like I'm hiding in a women's rest room."

Greg noticed the broken glass on the floor. George grinned. "Tech 3," he said. "The wife called her husband downtown. He didn't like it."

George kept a glass resting precariously on the water cooler. If a playback vibrated enough with an angry voice, the tremble would set the cooler to shaking and the glass would crash. A man could die of boredom riding a Tech if he couldn't indulge in such nonsense.

At Crime Lab, Greg asked for Grainger, a sound technician with an almost unholy reverence for his subject. He came forward, eyes squinting, hair rumpled, clothes sagging. His myopic eyes brightened when he was close enough to recognize Greg.

"You've got them?" he asked.

Greg nodded and handed him two reels of tape. "These are the voices I want checked against this one"—he tapped the second reel—"which is Hoagy's."

Grainger thought he could complete the test in six hours. He would telephone Greg at once if an ident was made. . . .

The desk clerk cast a supercilious glance Greg's way as Greg entered an old Tudor apartment house whose atmosphere was that of expensive decadence. At Suite 110, Joe Packer opened the door to his knock.

"It's a good setup," Packer said. He nodded toward a technician at the far end of the living room who was installing a 16-mm. movie camera. With him was Sanders, a wiry, five-foot-three expert on bugs, who was more at home in the labyrinthine blackness between the floors of a building than in a living room full of people. Greg had never heard his first name. Everyone called him Termie, short for Termite.

At the "window" Greg looked into a living room that was a period piece with soft pastel drapes. The walls were a formal

54

gray. A door to the right admitted on a hall which midway led to a dining room and, at the far end, to two bedrooms.

The plan, as they had outlined it to Lancaster, was to take sound motion pictures of Malone talking with Ellen Marshall whenever the conversation might possibly concern the movement of money. Perhaps they might get the full story on film, which would be tantamount to a confession when shown in court. If not that, then they might obtain leads.

"It's a neat setup," Termie agreed, "except that our contact mike won't work. It'll pull through a two-foot wall, usually, but there's some electrical disturbance in there."

"Means we've got to bug the room?" Greg asked. Termie nodded.

"I don't like it——" Packer began, and stopped short. Greg, who had been tinkering with a camera, turned to glance through the "window." Ellen Marshall was walking toward them from the hall, and they had the strange feeling they should duck, that surely she would see them.

She was too tall and too dark and admitted it frankly. She stood straight as an arrow and let her long legs sway her hips in the natural, sensuous way of an island native. An uncluttered dress the color of dry champagne pointed up her olive skin and black hair and detracted not a whit from her tall grace.

As she approached, her glance darted about the room in final inspection. She appeared to be singing softly to herself from the way her lips moved. It was like an old-time silent movie, since they had not yet installed a microphone.

Coming to a stop before the mirror not more than a foot away, she looked straight at them. Greg had a strange, uneasy feeling, as always. She studied herself critically and appeared satisfied with what she saw. She raised her arms to arrange her hair at the back. She was so close they could see the shadow of the freshly shaved armpits.

"I think if we plant the bug behind the baseboard over there," Packer said, unconsciously lowering his voice to a whisper, "and fish the wire between the studs . . ."

She bent over and ran a finger test up the thin seam of her nylons. Then she plumped up the pillows of the sofa, explored the surface of the lamp table for dust, and strolled back to the bedroom.

They walked away from the "window." Packer said, "About eleven, then?" and Greg nodded. They would bug her apartment while she and Malone were at a night club.

Shortly afterward he returned to headquarters and was hurrying down the dark, tunnel-like corridor of the first floor when Akers called to him. Akers handed him the memo of a phone message that read: "Mrs. James H. Roberts, 1935 East Carroll Street, telephoned at 1:43 P.M. to advise she had read in the newspapers about police efforts to locate Sharon 'Cokie' Logan. She advised that her daughter, Gale Roberts, was the unknown girl friend of the newspaper account who was accompanying Miss Logan. She advised furthermore that the two girls had planned to stop at Ocean Beach for two days and then proceed to Lake Little Bear. She advised she had had a postcard from her daughter from Ocean Beach."

As he finished, he heard Akers saying, "We've asked the sheriff's office to contact their deputy at Arrowview. He covers the Little Bear area."

Greg handed the memo back, a warm feeling suffusing him.

At the first pay phone he called Cyn. "Yes, I fed Mr. Adam," she said in that bubbly, teasing tone of hers, "and for your information, Mr. Evans, I don't think he's your cat any more. He's packed his fur and moved over."

CHAPTER 10

Gale, wallpaper-clad in a white turtle-neck and red skirt, steered a course through the jam-packed tables to the far end of the dining room. Cokie, in similar uniform, followed. Before sitting down Gale paused momentarily to case the room with an expert eye.

"Well?" inquired Cokie.

"No," Gale reported flatly. "And us all gussied up." She sat down disgustedly. Cokie fingered the little silver cross at her throat. Gale frowned. Cokie always looked as though she were enjoying a secret joke.

"What happened to the college man in the blue jeans and big brown eyes," Gale wanted to know, "in the short time it took me to fill up a sweater and get back here?"

Cokie grinned. "I saw him giving a line to that brunette in the yellow dress with the black stripes going around."

"*That* wasp?"

"Honestly, Gale, you're going to pick up the wrong fellow sometime." Cokie sobered. Unconsciously she had used the very words that Julia Bunker downstairs had said about Jan once. She loathed the woman and categorically refused to believe a word she said.

Jan's face, as they had driven away that morning, kept haunting her. She had watched her turn back toward the apartment after saying good-by, noticed the stiff, automatic smile drop away and the haggard, glazed look settle back in place.

They split the check, with Cokie owing Gale two cents. Afterwards they drifted to the pier, where they rented a rowboat. The sunset's afterglow was only a wisp. As Gale pushed the boat away and settled down to row, the unreal quiet of dusk was broken only by the faint rhythmic put-put of an outboard far away.

The gentle, cradling sway of the boat was lulling. For a long time they said nothing, listening to the soft splash of the oars in the water and the last good night of a bird in flight.

When they eventually started talking again, it was about the usual subject. "Do you really expect that log pusher to join us?" Gale asked.

"Um-uum."

"What d'you see in that Mick Foster?"

"You just look at men, Gale. You don't understand them."

"And you do."

"Look. He never had anyone. His aunt and uncle raised him and they didn't care much for him. He's never had any real affection. I mean, real love. It was this—this feeling of insecurity, this —this need for affection, that was why——"

"Gosh, what I missed not taking Psych IV. You gonna give him security?"

"I am."

Gale could just see her, jaw set and mind, too. She was so positive about everything. No doubts, no hesitation, whether it was dating a boy or picking a dress. Gale whispered softly, "Oh, brother!"

"You'll see." Again the rebel toss of hair.

"Not in my lifetime." Cokie's silence was more eloquent than words. Gale could not endure it for long. "Cokie," she said contritely, "if Mick's all right with you, he's all right with me. And I don't care what Jan says. She hasn't any right to talk, anyway— dating that bone crusher. What's his name?"

"The Panther. Golly, I miss him. He used to help me wax the car." He also had given her tickets to his matches, and she had organized a co-ed fan club with the slogan, "Pant with Panther," which her English lit prof said was so nauseous he had to take dramamine every time he heard it.

"Miss him? Isn't he around any more?"

"No—Dr. Jones came along. You know, the nuclear physicist who gave the talk at assembly."

"Don't tell me Jan's the mental type. Why, if I had a body around like the Panther's——"

"Gale!"

"Well, if I had I'd let someone else crack the atom."

Dr. C. Oxford Jones was his full name. She never had gotten around to asking what the C. stood for. Probably something like Clancy. But if she were going to fall in love with an "older man," she would have chosen Dr. Jones—nuclear physics, Clancy, and all. He was tall, well built, and his hair had a graying touch that verified his learning. He had, moreover, the most soothing voice she ever hoped to hear, and it seemed when he looked at you he was talking to no one else.

"He's positively nylon," she said.

Gale was disgusted. "Cokie, you like everyone."

They fell silent. The put-put that had been a background noise increased rapidly in volume, like a record turned up sharply. A racing motorboat was bearing toward them, its light cutting a sharp, bright, triangular lane through the dark that had fallen with surprising suddenness. "Those darn fools," Gale said. "Have you had enough?"

As she turned the boat about, the outboard roared past them, setting their boat to rocking. A couple of young fellows waved in high hilarity. "Darn fools," Gale repeated.

After they tied up, they returned to the lodge, where Gale bought a couple of pennants at the curio counter for her younger brother. The college man in blue jeans sauntered up as she was paying, and the pennants were good for conversation. A few minutes later she returned to Cokie and said, "I've got a date to go riding. Mind if I run out on you?"

Cokie smiled. "It's your life," she said.

After they were gone, she read in the lounge. She was so lost in a magazine story that when she finally looked up she discovered she was alone and it was a little after eleven.

As she started down the road, she passed a teen-age couple strolling awkwardly with their arms about each other. She felt a hungry longing to have Mick's arms about her, feel his rough lips pressing hers. It was that kind of a night. The stars were low, like rhinestone clusters, and across the lake there spread a lighted fairyland on a ribbon. The waves lapped in mood music, and occasionally a bird would talk in his sleep.

On another night she would have reveled dreamily in all this, but little things kept pressing and nudging. Like the night she awakened frightened, the phone ringing. Jan was already out of bed. She heard her say in a low voice that didn't sound like Jan, "I've told you. Don't call me again." Jan had banged down the receiver. When she returned she said, "Some drunk." But she hadn't slept the rest of the night.

A car's lights were two eyes far down the road, looking toward her. They swelled as they approached very slowly, and then she and the woods about her were caught up in a flooding spotlight. She glanced away to avoid the blinding glare. The eyes seemed to look her over until they were quite near, and then on impulse they shot past her, so fast they left a breeze in their wake that whipped about her.

She grew conscious shortly afterward that someone was walking down the road behind her, his cigarette a firefly dot, his footsteps padded. Everything again was silent and dark, like black velvet. She moved farther to the side of the road and slowed her pace. When he came even, she saw it wasn't a "he" at all. It was a woman in levis.

Cokie left the highway at a wagon-wheel marker, taking a foot path across a brook to a cabin set deep in the woods. It was one of a cluster, all dark.

As she opened the door, she hesitated and stood very still, listening. She thought she had heard a movement inside. She realized then she couldn't have, because the brook was too noisy. Still, she threw the flashlight about, past the beaten-up dressing table, the low double bed with its faded, patched spread, the lone straight chair, and hence to the bathroom door, slightly ajar.

She took a step toward the light cord dangling in the center of the room. In the same fleeting second she smelled the alien tobacco and heard the faint swift movement behind her and the door closing. As she whirled about, a sharp hard blow snapped her wrist. The flashlight crashed to the floor, the glass shattering, and went out. A scream of pain rose to her lips, where it was blotted out by a hand thrust roughly against her mouth. An arm slipped about her middle, crushing her hands to her sides and getting a strangle hold on her.

She jerked her head back and brought her teeth down on the hand. She was thrown violently against the dresser, which collapsed and went down with her.

She screamed. A blow caught her on the jaw, knifing the sound off. Hands grabbed her and dragged her roughly to her feet, a cloth was ramrodded between her teeth, and again an arm was crushing her, shutting off her breath until she thought she would black out.

She heard people talking . . . *I thought I heard a woman scream . . . Me too . . . Oh, come back to bed, Jim, it was an animal . . . They tell me there's a bird sounds like that . . . I don't hear anything . . .*

She was dragged toward the door. Her body was part of another body, pressed close, moving with it. She was choking, gasping, her throat dry and burning. She lurched violently and caught the arm off guard. She let flail with her fists, and then as the arm closed about her again, she brought a knee up into a soft groin. There was the low moan of deep pain.

Voices were outside the door. *I tell you, I do hear something.*

She was thrown against the wall. She cowered, expecting a blow. She heard the movement through the window, the movement at the door, and then the light was striking her eyes, and a couple of men in robes were standing over her, and there was a woman, and three children.

CHAPTER 11

As Greg sped along the waterfront to the Harbor Street gym to interview Panther Wilson, the wrestler, his thoughts were on planting the mike that night in Ellen Marshall's apartment. He ran swiftly over the possible hazards, the dangers that beset every talking-bug job. They must have a lookout outside the apartment building to warn them if she and Malone returned unexpectedly. They would slip in the back door with a passkey supplied by the building manager and hence should have a chart of the rear area, including the alley, so they might avoid being seen by any neighbor chancing to glance out a window. They would work in the dark, because a light in the apartment might be noticed by someone passing along the hall who knew Ellen Marshall was gone.

If despite every precaution they were trapped, they would pretend they were private detectives and would offer identification carrying fake names and addresses. The department, of course, would disclaim all responsibility, if somehow their true identities were discovered, and would suspend them for conduct unbecoming an officer.

It was this furtiveness, this concealment, this being a police officer and not being one, this "breaking and entering" like a thug, that bothered him. And sometimes it would jar him awake in the dead of the night when a man's inner self looks his actions squarely in the face. Even the quiver of excitement he felt now, induced by the adventure and danger he would run tonight, was the kind a burglar must feel when he slips through the dark.

He told himself he was acting the fool. This bug he would plant tonight might solve the death of the little Blatt boy in St. Louis, or the shotgun blasting of the girl bank teller in Phoenix, or any of a dozen heinous cases. And he had no complaint with the Tech operation as set up by Lancaster, who followed a policy adhered to by most police departments—a policy that permitted taps and bugs only in crimes of extreme bestial violence, such as murder and threats to murder, kidnapings, extortions, gangland operations, aggravated assault, rape, and the like.

He found a parking space near the gym and, crossing the street, knew he was marked by the hangers-on as either a police officer, a bill collector, a newspaperman, or a lawyer. They eyed him with indifference and arrogance and belligerence, depending on whether they were has-beens or young hopefuls or well-dressed toughs or hoodlums biding their time until nightfall, when they would knock over a cigar store or waylay a girl.

A juke box was blaring inside and the pinball machines were click-clicking away. Some twenty feet farther, at the door to the gym, a sign read: "No Visitors Today—Workouts."

He walked past the sign and pushed the doors open. A man's bellow caught up with him. "Hey, slugger, where you going?" The man merely grunted when he showed his badge.

Inside the gym, he could smell the hotness of naked bodies struggling on the big mat. "Where'll I find Panther?" he asked a fellow reading a racing form.

"Straight ahead, second room," he answered without looking up.

As Greg passed the ring, he heard a wrestler say, "Give me that foot in the face the way you did in Frisco."

At the second door he knocked and walked in. A big heavy-set man was being given an alcohol rub on a table. Greg said, "I'm looking for Panther Wilson."

The big fellow rolled over on his back. "I'm Panther," he said, raising his head to see Greg. His block shoulders filled the table. He was drifting into his late forties, still a handsome man in a rugged, chiseled fashion.

"You a newspaper guy?" he asked with interest.

"Not quite," Greg answered, showing him his badge. "Could we talk alone?"

The rubber turned to leave. "Stay where you are, Beer Barrel," Panther ordered, swinging agilely into a sitting position. "You're wasting your time," he said to Greg.

Greg felt the blood in his face. "One of your friends has drowned," he said evenly. "We're trying to find her sister."

Panther stood up, taking a hitch at his shorts. "I don't talk to cops."

The rubber laughed nervously, like a punch-drunk.

Greg said, "Look—I don't care what you think about cops. Where's Cokie Logan?"

Panther turned away, picking up a turkish towel. He had a Buddha stomach, and one quick hard blow to the navel would double him up.

"You heard me," Panther said, rubbing so hard the blood surfaced. "Show him where the door is, Beer Barrel."

Greg's look stopped him. Beer Barrel laughed again.

Greg turned back to Panther. "You don't like me and I don't like you. So that's settled. So where's Cokie Logan?"

Greg was telling himself, I mustn't let him nettle me. A detective's no good if he lets his emotions ride him—a monkey on his back. That's what they taught you in police school, a pretty speech that one hot surge of blood could blot out.

He said coolly, "You dated Jan Logan. You took her to your wrestling matches, to crummy night clubs. Maybe she was only something flashy to wear on your arm."

He saw Panther breathing hard. "But if she was something you cared a little for—well, she's dead, and we want to find her kid sister."

Panther put on a shirt and buttoned it slowly, a shirt with a two-inch "W" monogram. Greg shrugged and walked to the door. "He's all yours, Beer Barrel," he said. "Rub him down and embalm him good."

He could scarcely see as he left the gym. His blood was too much at times for this business.

He was trying to figure out the why of Panther Wilson when he walked into the Tech Room. The churning inside had slowed a little, but not much.

George Benson came out of his chair. He seemed to think he should be standing when Greg was around. "They don't give Joan much of a chance," he said. "She's in a coma now." He said it as if she were his little girl, and Greg knew the man's warmth and heart for the first time, although they had worked together for six months. It took something like this to bring a man out.

"God," Greg said.

George cleared his throat. "A couple of girls on Tech 15 discussed their boy friends. I typed it up myself and stamped it obscene."

He continued, "Old 66 just quit gushing. Not much on it. Want me to play it back?"

He strung the tape on another machine. They listened as Hoagy and Malone talked, at first mostly about Malone's mother, who had had a bad fall. Malone was broken up about it, and for the first time Greg heard the thin, listless voice come alive. It took something to bring a man out, he thought again.

George said, "Here it comes." And then:

"Have you heard any more about the deal?" It was Malone's voice.

"Zump says it's all set. He'll keep me posted."

"Good. I'll notify the bank to deliver the money at the usual place."

The conversation then returned to Malone's mother. Greg went into his office, feeling low. They had not mentioned Cokie Logan. If 66 should garbo out on them . . .

Nor had the Malmo detail succeeded in identifying Zump. The FBI had been requested to run an indices check on its criminal name file in Washington. It was an odd name, and something might come of it.

His call to Homicide was delayed a few minutes. When he did get through, he learned that Cokie Logan and her girl friend, Gale Roberts, had checked out of the Little Bear lodge. Not only had the Arrowview deputy failed to locate them, but he was not at all hopeful. His area contained thirty-seven resorts, jammed with around ten thousand holiday guests. Some of the resorts, he said, were operated "family-style" and never bothered to register guests.

Greg sat thinking a long time, jotting down the leads in both the Malmo and Jan Logan cases, which probably were related, and wondering which ones should be checked out first. It was always like that in police work. A detective had forty leads he could work, forty leads that might take weeks. He started with those he thought the most promising, and then if it were the thirty-first that worked out, everyone asked why the stupid police hadn't done that in the beginning.

It was like drilling oil wells. A man sank so many dry holes before he hit a gusher. And sometimes he never did.

The phone rang at his elbow, startling him. It was Grainger, the sound man. "I've got a possible ident for you," he said. "I think I know who Hoagy is. Can you come over?"

Grainger was pleased. He had two movie projectors set up side by side in his cubbyhole office.

"Sit here," he said, indicating the chair behind the desk. "This was interesting—very interesting, indeed. I needn't go into details because I know you are interested only in the results. I will say this—that sound, as you probably know, is nothing more than vibrations of the air that hit the ears, and that when we put sound on film we merely translate these air vibrations into electrical ones and come up with a varying band of light on the film."

He switched out the overhead lights. "So I am going to project these voices as shadows—not as sounds. You won't hear anything. I have photographed the sound—so to speak—and this is what we have."

He started a projector, with an image about a foot wide falling on the bare wall.

"I have chosen the tape marked Dr. C. Oxford Jones," he said. "You will please note that the shadows form a fairly regular pattern of peaks and valleys, indicating that he talks along smoothly without unduly raising his voice. We call it plateau speech, or on a plane."

The film took but a minute. While he was fumbling around, trying to rewind it, he continued with his explanation. "Everyone's speech has valleys and peaks. No one talks completely on a plateau—probably couldn't even if he tried."

He interrupted himself. "What's wrong here? I never could cope with machinery."

Greg found the rewind switch and threw it. "I take it," he said, "that Dr. Jones is not Hoagy."

"Not at all—not at all. But here he is."

With Greg's help, he threaded the film. The image, even to Greg's untrained eyes, was different.

"It's bong, bong, bong, bong," said Grainger. "The peaks are high and occur at irregular intervals, creating a jagged, distinctive pattern. We don't find it too often. This man hits his words like they were nails."

66

Greg picked up the tape can. The identification was Ed Anderson—Ed Anderson, the used-car dealer who had been a friend of Jan Logan.

"I will run both projectors simultaneously," Grainger said. "The one on the right will carry the voice identified as Hoagy's."

"Well, I'll be——" said Greg as he watched the shadows dance in almost identical patterns in the two images.

Grainger switched the lights back on. "I should warn you," he said, "that this is not a science—I mean not a positive one—the way fingerprints are."

He spoke as though he did not believe it. "It is intended only as a suggestion. In this case, however, I don't think you will find an error."

On his way back to Tech, Greg stopped at Kirk's Sport Shop, which served as headquarters for the Snorkel Whippers, the skin divers' club, and asked to see the membership list. He recognized one name, that of Panther Wilson. He had joined the club five months before, and his sponsor had been Jan Logan.

CHAPTER 12

Jesse Taylor leaned back. He'd show them. He'd steal five minutes every hour from them. Let the tomcat phone ring.

They expected you to keep the books, and answer the fool questions people with nothing to do thought up, and hand out the mail, and peddle cigarettes and candy, and see that Bessie straight-ended up the cottages proper-like, and keep track of who was where, and the keys, and don't let the fishermen bring their bait, and admonish the little gangsters.

The five minutes up, clocked to a second, he picked up the receiver. "Where in thunderation you been, Jess?" the voice said, jovial-like, but Jesse felt his hackles rising. The name was Jesse, not Jess.

It was that young Bill Marks, the deputy at Arrowview. He was always telling Mary that that young Marks couldn't catch an elephant in a telephone booth.

"I got something to do besides answer the blasted phone," he shouted back.

Bill wanted to know if a couple of young women were registered, one Miss Logan and one Miss Roberts. Jesse picked up the card before him. Yes, those were the names. They had paid up a few minutes ago and checked out. Maybe, if Bill would hold on, he could catch them.

He made his way across the lodge room as fast as his arthritic joints would permit, colliding inevitably with a space-man who couldn't see whether he was coming or going.

He saw the car moving away as he stepped out on the porch. "Hey!" he shouted. Everybody turned around all the way to the lake. "Hey!" he yelled again, waving, and tottering down the steps. The car was too far away for the girls to hear him, he realized, and turned back.

Well, it probably didn't matter. Bill Marks was always fussing around with stolen tires and that kind of truck. The time they did have a shooting—when that drunk said he was Billy the Kid and the other said he wasn't—Bill Marks was on vacation.

What would Bill want them two kids for, anyway? They were pretty as molasses. One was dreamy and the other, her motor was running all the time. They couldn't have been more than twenty. Girls sure filled out fast these days. He remembered when he'd married old bones and slats . . .

"They're gone," he announced cryptically over the phone.

"Which way they heading?" Bill asked.

Jesse hesitated. Come to think of it, he hadn't waited to see which turnoff they took from the crossroads.

"They took the Chase road," he said emphatically. Bill wasn't going to catch him napping. Maybe they had, and if Bill didn't find them on it, then maybe they had turned back and struck off in another direction. Nobody could prove anything.

"Thanks, Jess," Bill said, and hung up, all in a hurry.

The Chase road was a good choice. It ran fifty-eight miles across the hills to Lake Robinhood. It had more branches than a setting hen eggs.

It'd give Bill Marks something to do.

CHAPTER 13

Greg attempted to simulate casualness as he walked into Hoagy Anderson's office. Lancaster had suggested he "drop in" on Anderson on the pretext of trying to locate Cokie Logan and size up the man and the place. Under no circumstances was he to ask questions that might stir suspicion. For the first time in his seven years with the department he had written out the questions and memorized them.

Lancaster had repeated, "I don't care how much evidence you get against Anderson, I don't want him picked up until we've got the same evidence on Malone. It's Malone we're after. He alone's got the money to float an operation like this."

Before Greg left headquarters, he had run the indices at Records and come up with a "no make"—that is, Records had no criminal record on Edward Osten Anderson, at least not under that name. Records had promised they would request an "answer today sure" FBI check. He had learned at City Credit, where he stopped en route to the used-car lot, that Anderson had had seventeen suits and liens filed against him the last two years for nonpayment of debts and that his risk rating was "poor." The credit report indicated, however, that the used-car lot was a going business operation and not a blind.

Greg was convinced further when he walked on the lot, which had the usual signs, "Come In—Kick Our Tires" and "Nothing

Down—Years to Pay." Although it was the dinner hour, he counted a score of customers roaming about, inspecting cars that ranged from one-hundred-dollar jalopies to four-thousand-dollar Jaguars.

The office was in dead center and glassed on all sides. Anderson could see over the lot without moving from his desk. He was talking with a customer when Greg entered.

"Hello there," he said. "Sit down and I'll be right with you."

He was a mastiff of a man, with a mastiff's face, rugged and beaten, and with skin like old meerschaum. He was carrying on an intelligible conversation, although it was evident his mind was doing a comptometering job elsewhere. He had a pencil gripped tightly.

He said to Greg again, "I'll be right with you." The customer, though, hung on tenaciously, seeking to learn the history of the car he was buying, whether it had ever been in an accident, and harried by the usual doubts of a man purchasing a secondhand automobile.

Greg studied the scene outside. He spotted, across the street, the two men Lancaster had assigned to run a tail job. He reached the obvious conclusion that the surveillance would yield little. In a day's time Hoagy Anderson probably talked with a hundred people. It would be impossible to run checks on them all, to find out which ones were the "they" who had slain Jan and planned to murder Cokie, and to identify the "Zump" of the $400,000 money highjacking plot.

"If anything goes wrong, bring it in, Mr. Bascomb," Hoagy said at the door. "You never have to worry when you buy here."

He turned back. "Sorry to keep you waiting. Sit here." He indicated the chair across from his desk. "What can I do for you?"

Greg moved with deliberation. Hoagy's unexpected approach, his unbridled heartiness, had thrown him slightly off balance.

"I'm Greg Evans," he said. "From the police."

"Excuse me one minute, Evans." Hoagy flicked on the intercom, and his logger's voice fairly burst a loud-speaker outside. "Champ, come to the office."

He swung around to Greg. "Sorry."

"We understand you were a friend of Jan Logan's," Greg said.

"Yeah, that's right. Jan and I did some dating. Not much. Went to the races, did some drinking together, that kind of business, you know."

Greg nodded. "Well, actually we weren't interested in that." He let the point establish itself and then continued, "We want to find her sister to let her know."

Champ came in. "You want me, boss?"

"Yes, Champ. I saw that '52 DeSoto cream puff come back. What's wrong?"

"The kid says the motor block's cracked."

"How about it?"

"The overhaul card doesn't show it."

"Give him his money back."

"He wants another car."

"Give him his money back and tell him to go down the street."

In the same breath he said to Greg, "I never met Cokie. Don't know her at all."

Greg brought his long frame up out of the chair. "Well, thanks, Mr. Anderson. We thought you might—or that Jan Logan might have mentioned where her sister was going."

"Have you tried Bill Buller? Jan worked for him, you know."

He walked to the door with Greg. "I remember when I first saw Jan. She came in here to buy a car. Bought a '51 Oldsmobile straw hat, a sweet little number. The next time I saw her was when I dropped into the Champagne Room and we hit up a conversation. She was okay."

Greg remarked, "In these drowning cases, we always have to consider the suicide angle."

Hoagy shrugged. "I guess you never know what goes on inside anybody. We're all mystery stories—even to ourselves."

He flipped a cigarette stub out the door. "Next time you want a car, drop around. I'll make you a good price."

Greg said, "Thanks, Mr. Anderson," and "It looks like we might have a shower," and then was walking across the lot, carrying away the impression that Hoagy Anderson purposely had told more than he needed to.

CHAPTER 14

Until a little after ten Greg read the typed transcripts on the day's techs, routing the pertinent ones to the proper squads. A tap on a narcotics case appeared the most promising. A wholesaler of marihuana was due to arrive the next day with one hundred thousand cigarettes for a dealer who peddled retail to Babcock High School students. The tech had come up with the place and time of delivery.

He poked along with the slow outbound traffic in driving to Ellen Marshall's apartment building. He did his best thinking when he was driving—although Judge Jones of Traffic Court had a lecture for his kind.

He let himself into the Malmo apartment with a dupe key and joined Packer and Termie, the bug expert, at the "window."

Packer glanced at his watch. "Ten twenty-five. Malone's never late."

They stepped down from the "window." Packer continued, "The grapevine has it the grand jury's after us."

"That's what I hear."

Packer said with irritation, "Why's everyone so excited about phone tapping? Everybody listens in on your line anyway. It's the great American sport. I've got a couple of teen-agers on my line——"

"Some people don't see it that way."

"What're they complaining about?"

"Well, among other things, they figure we're listening to the innocent as well as the guilty when we put on a tap—and then, also, they think it violates the idea no man can be forced to testify against himself. On a tap, of course, he may incriminate himself."

Packer shrugged. "I don't go for all this good sportsmanship when it comes to criminals. The next thing you know we'll have a closed season on 'em."

Termie called to them, and through the "window" they saw Ellen Marshall open the eighteenth-century panel doors to a built-in record player. After starting it she moved away, swaying a little, presumably to the music. She was in a black evening dress that revealed her well-disciplined body and the outline of her lingerie. Malone had libeled her when he said she was spreading.

She lit a long cigarette, her movements precise and definite, and walked straight toward them, to the mirror. Her dress was off the shoulder, and she studied it a moment. She lowered it until it was quite revealing, but decided against it.

Again, of course, the scene was a silent one, but they knew there had been a tap on the door when she swung in that direction. She drew in a deep breath, like an athlete readying himself for the showdown, and put on an inviting smile. She turned the overhead lights out, leaving only a table lamp in a far corner.

Malone, with every hair in its proper place, walked into her arms. She kissed him almost savagely, but his reaction was that of a man who has known a woman for so many years that her embraces are about as interesting as putting on his socks. She pressed her body against his, as though unsure of herself. When she let go of him, she turned quickly toward the mirror, and Greg thought he saw something like fury in her eyes. Malone took quick inventory of his suit and came to the mirror to remove the lipstick and restore a couple of hairs to their assigned positions. In the meantime she disappeared, reappearing with a mink and her own lipstick job repaired. She turned off the lamp as they left.

"I don't know about that room," Termie said. "It looks hot to me. We may get some bounce out of it."

"Well, we could knock a wall out," Greg said, grinning, and Termie laughed. He was dressed as a telephone repairman.

"Where's my rat hole?" he asked. He walked with the other two away from the "window."

"It's at the far end of the hall—as far as you can go," Packer told him.

"We got lookouts on this one?"

Greg nodded. "Packer's covering the back door and we've got a couple men out front."

Termie picked up a stepladder and slung a reel of wire over his shoulder. Greg walked down the corridor with him, while Packer left for the back of the building to begin his watch. Termie put the ladder up to the square opening in the ceiling—the opening to a twelve-inch clearance between the floors. Once he had climbed into the clearance, Greg took the ladder away, and Termie pulled the board back across the opening to close it. He would now squirm through the narrow clearance until he was over Ellen Marshall's apartment.

After returning the ladder to the Malmo apartment, Greg left the building by the front entrance. As he passed the switchboard desk he recognized the officer in plain clothes sitting in a lobby chair, pretending to read a magazine. Another officer was strolling along the street outside, but he also passed Greg without a greeting.

Greg followed the block around until he came to the alley, then walked briskly down it, counting the rear doors. The fourth would be hers. It was the usual city alley, paved and dotted with garbage cans, with flowerpots in some of the windows and dishrags drying in others. He crossed one swatch of light falling from the second story, heard faintly a Strauss waltz, and caught the odor of minestrone mixed with a night flower.

He slipped the passkey in and worked feverishly with it. It was a dupe, and a dupe of a passkey could never be trusted. At a faint movement in the shrubs back of him, across the alleyway, he stood rigid. He hoped it was Packer; he was almost certain it was; but anyway, he couldn't stop now.

His fingers were "feeling" the key, and the door opened at last to his touch. After closing it behind him, he stood motionless, listening intently, and in a moment knew he was alone. The place had that deathly stillness.

74

He switched on his flashlight only enough to guide him from the service room through the kitchen, into the dining area, thence into the hall and the living room. He had moved smoothly, on muscles basketball-trained, with the deep carpeting absorbing his light footfalls.

At the east wall he knelt, his hands running swiftly and expertly over the baseboard. Before he started working, he knocked twice at the spot where he intended to place the bug, and in a moment an answering tap came from the ceiling overhead. It was uncanny how Termie could find his way so accurately between the floors when he had nothing to guide him.

With experienced hands Greg pried the baseboard loose from the wall with a screwdriver, backing the screwdriver with a piece of cloth so he would leave no telltale marks on the plaster. He loosened a section of board about eight feet long and easily lifted it out.

His whole body galvanized when he heard footsteps stop outside the corridor door. The muted voices of two men came over in a low surreptitious tone. He waited, every muscle taut, in the kneeling position the voices had caught him in. He wondered about the lookout. And then the footsteps picked up their natural cadence, moving down the corridor, and he sagged.

From his back trousers pocket he took the bug, a crystal mike a little larger than a dollar and several times thicker. It looked a little like the disk inside a telephone receiver. He felt around for the fish wire that Termie had dropped down, to tie the bug wire to. As his hands explored between the studs they came in contact with a small round object like the one he was installing.

Someone else already had bugged the room.

It might be an old bug, planted years before and never removed, or it could be a new one.

He was tempted to snip its lead wire, but then if it were a "live" one, the party owning it would investigate and discover the police microphone. So he decided to leave it. Tomorrow Termie could trace it to its source by following its lead wire.

He knocked on the wall three times to signal for Termie to pull up the bug's wire. When it was tight, he anchored the bug solidly, making certain its "ear" was turned toward the room, and started to replace the baseboard.

It was then he heard Packer's low warning whistle outside the window.

The dull groaning of wood on wood as the back door rubbed the sill came over distinctly. . . .

Termie pulled the "fish" up until he had hold of the bug's lead wire. He then untied the "fish," rolled it up, and stuck it in his hip pocket.

He already had discovered the connecting cord from the other bug. It ran straight ahead of him, as far as his flashlight carried, veering slightly toward the building's outside wall. He suspected the "planter" probably had run it out of the building and was monitoring it from another apartment house. It could be a federal government bug or a private detective's. It might belong to the sheriff's men, although this was city territory. He had caught them before, though, trying to sneak mikes into police jurisdiction in the hope of stealing a beat on a big case. If this was a sheriff's bug, he would like to cut the connection and then lie in wait for their man to come along trouble shooting. He would conk him one and later say he thought he was a private detective.

He crawled away, unwinding the lead wire as he did, and laying it across the boards. He slithered like a snake, since the crossbeams in spots were so low he had little room even for his elbows. Most men would have felt entombed, but here, burrowing mole-like through the blackness, he was at peace with his thoughts, the world utterly shut out. There were noises, of course, drifting from above and below, but they were dull, unrecognizable sounds that had had the stridency filtered out of them. Even the sticky sweat that was soaking his shirt was nostalgic, and the hot still air that didn't seem air at all, and the cooking smells, funneled together.

As he squirmed along, he counted the studs until he was sure he was at the outside Malmo apartment wall, where he would drop the wire. Snapping off the flashlight, he lay quietly, waiting for

Greg's quick sharp knocks. He would place the knocks when they came, and make his "incision," and drop the wire. He took pride he was never more than a foot off. For twelve years now he had been the police department's bug man, listed on the pay roll as a radio technician. Only once had he almost erred. That was the time he was crawling through the clearance over an auditorium in an ancient building. Suddenly he had felt the ceiling under him give a little, and in another second, would have crashed through, plummeting straight into a convention of the Daughters of the American Revolution. He laughed low to himself as he thought of it now. What consternation that would have caused among the Daughters!

He wondered what was taking Greg Evans so long. . . .

Greg heard the cautious tread of shoes across the kitchen linoleum. The footsteps died away in a second, absorbed by the carpeting. Quickly he pocketed the screwdriver and fitted the baseboard into place. The next he heard was heavy asthmatic breathing in the hall.

He pressed his body flat against the wall beside a period-piece secretary. He tried to still his breathing. He was conscious of a form moving by him out of the hall, a heavy form, judging by the slight give of the floor. A light came on unexpectedly, a table lamp.

The man's back was to him, bending low over the table. He was a huge man in a gray Donegal tweed. He turned about slowly and evenly. His face was out of the light, but his glasses caught a reflection. He stood there a moment, stock-still, glancing about the room without moving his pachyderm body, as though he had been here before and was surveying it to determine if anything was missing or had been added. His eyes passed lightly over the secretary, which was beyond the throw of the direct light and clothed with shadows.

Greg heard once more the low, surreptitious brush of shoes against the kitchen linoleum, and the man, too, heard. His eyes stopped their course and he listened, but decided he was mistaken. He moved his big form then across the room, walking toward the secretary. Greg waited, tense.

The man opened the secretary, so close that Greg could have touched him, and still seemed unaware of his presence. He took a stack of envelopes out of a drawer and turned as if to take them back to the light. Then he whirled, and with a powerful sweeping uppercut caught Greg dead on the chin. The snap of bone hitting bone cracked through the room. As the pain stung through him, the man swung again, but this time Greg deflected the blow in a sharp thrust of his left. He raised his knee as the huge form tore into him, and sent him tottering back, and swiftly followed up with a right hook that had the impact of a shot, and another right that tore into the soft underbelly. The man groaned and bent up and caved slowly to the floor.

It all happened in the time it took Packer to reach the living room. Greg stood a moment, stunned, and feeling his jaw.

"You all right?" Packer asked, and Greg nodded. "He had a passkey," Packer added.

Greg went through the man's pockets until he found his wallet. The man was breathing so laboriously he could be heard over the apartment.

Taking the wallet to the table light, Greg found the driver's license and read, "George Pierson—2398 Sun Lane." Packer jotted the facts down, and Greg returned the wallet.

"What'll we do with him?" Packer asked.

"Leave him," Greg said. He took a tack hammer from his pocket and tapped the baseboard flush with the wall. He played his flashlight over the nail holes to make certain he hadn't disturbed the paint.

"Let's get out of here." The throb in his jaw was pounding harder with each minute.

They locked the back door behind them and went around the block to the front entrance. After arranging with the two lookouts to run a tail job on the intruder when he came to, they went direct to the Malmo apartment to watch him. Packer took up vigil by the "window" while Greg tapped on a wall in signal to Termie, removed the baseboard, pulled in the lead wire, and connected it to a playback. He was putting the board back in place when Packer called.

They watched as the man sat up. He looked as if he were trying to fit the pieces together. With great effort he got to his feet. And then, after disappearing down the hall, apparently to see if his assailant was still lurking somewhere, he returned to the living room, straightened a chair that had been knocked down, picked up a magazine, arranged it just so, and smoothed out the rug.

CHAPTER 15

He lay awake a long time, thinking of the talking bugs and the one-way window into Ellen Marshall's apartment and the mike in the wall. A sentence he had read that day stayed with him. A newspaper columnist had quoted a Supreme Court justice as saying that "the greatest dangers to liberty lurk in the insidious encroachment by men of zeal."

He wondered, as he fell asleep, if he was one of those men of zeal.

It seemed as though he had barely dropped off when he heard a voice calling. Through foggy eyes the blurred picture of Cyn wavered in the open window across the room. Mr. Adam kicked then, and it was Mr. Adam who brought him finally awake. Mr. Adam slept at his feet, and if Greg moved too much in the night, Mr. Adam kicked.

"You'd think I was your wife," Cyn was saying. "Your phone's been ringing for fifteen minutes."

Lancaster was on the line. "We're in trouble," he said. "Mc-Tamish broke the Jan Logan story in the eight o'clock."

Greg came sharply awake. "Everything?"

"Just about. Will you see McTamish—see what you can do?" Lancaster read the story: "'The possibility that Jan Logan, twenty-eight-year-old realtor, may have been the victim of a bizarre murder plot unfolded today as high police sources confirmed they were investigating mysterious circumstances in connection with her death.

"'Miss Logan, a pretty statuesque one-time model——'"

Lancaster interrupted himself. "She worked as a model for six weeks once. McTamish is trying to make out she's Marilyn Monroe."

He continued with the news account. "'Miss Logan, a pretty statuesque one-time model, who was employed by the William C. Buller Realty Company, was drowned Monday night at Sandy Beach. Her death was listed on police records as accidental.

"'Police officers, acting on instructions from Assistant Chief Lancaster, admitted they had concealed the fact that three Homicide detectives were sent to Sandy Beach Monday night following a tip received from an unidentified informant who advised that 'somebody' had been killed.'"

Lancaster quit reading. "We've got to get McTamish to lay off. Tell him we'll give him the next big break. And, Evans—you got to get him to keep it off his midnight broadcast. More people listen to that than read the paper."

In every tavern in town the television was snapped off and the radio on when McTamish—in a breathless, two-seconds-to-live voice—began his "Crime Beat" broadcast. The night-club crowd and theatergoers and other stay-up-laters swore by him.

"Anything on the girl?" Greg asked.

"Nothing—but this story——"

"I know." The empty feeling was deep in him—and the alarm.

Lancaster added, "The highway patrol's running road blocks around Arrowview."

As Greg hung up, he noted his watch hands were turning toward nine. McTamish would be checking the courts soon. He whipped his fatigued, rebellious body into dressing and shaving, and left the cottage without having gotten breakfast for either himself or Mr. Adam.

At the Hall of Justice he stole a bailiff's parking space and bought an early edition as he entered the building. He thought, as he took the elevator, how the long cavernous stretches of the marble-floored halls must strike fear into people of simple lives who wandered here for the first time. Surely justice could be more approachable, something more than the product of a quarry.

He asked after McTamish in several offices before he trailed him to the corridor outside Superior Court No. 7, where he was talking with Henry Arnsten, the noted publicist. When he saw Greg, he nodded without losing a word the lawyer was saying. Greg waited out of earshot, leaning under an ancient portrait of a gloomy, long-forgotten chief justice.

A few moments later McTamish strolled over, penciling a note on folded copy paper as he did so. He stuck the copy paper in his breast pocket.

"Hello, Mac, can I talk with you a moment?"

McTamish took his time lighting a cigarette. "I thought you'd be around to see me," he said.

Greg studied his sated, intelligent face. Horace Greeley's estimate of Edgar Allan Poe fitted him well. "A brilliant writer when neither too drunk nor too sober." McTamish was too sober now.

"I've never asked you before, Mac——"

"The answer's no."

"Wait a minute, Mac. I want you to hear me out. I'm not denying the story's true."

McTamish looked at him in faint surprise. "Well, that's refreshing."

"It isn't that, Mac. You've stumbled on something—and you're giving it away to the killers. If you could wait a few days—we'll give you the whole story."

"I don't think Lancaster pays you enough for this kind of work."

Greg felt the anger in him. "I'll tell you the story—if it's off the record."

McTamish grinned. "I can get it on the record."

He put an arm on Greg's shoulders. "I like you, Greg. You know that. But it's an old record you're playing for Lancaster. Tell him I don't buy it."

"It's for a girl—a college kid you're triggering."

"I know, I know." He laughed to show Greg he wasn't taken in. "I'll tell you something a city editor once told me. No newspaper's ever a motive. The motive's already there. You know that."

He turned away. "I've got to be getting upstairs. The Howard divorce case's breaking. Eight women. It beats me how a man can find time."

Greg watched as he walked away, rolling slightly on an arthritic knee, his clothes like a detective's, not so well kept that they weren't ready for any job.

Greg walked down five flights of stairs to wear off the anger. He couldn't blame McTamish, but the Judas who had sold out the department to get his name in the paper . . .

He drifted into the coffee shop. But he couldn't finish his bacon and eggs, and the coffee burned his throat. He thumbed through a notebook until he located Dr. C. Oxford Jones and his address. Lancaster had taken him to task in his cold, polite way for having failed to interview Dr. Jones. Lancaster drove hard.

At the address he found a small residential hotel of sixteen or eighteen rooms. It was neat in a proper way, from the well-swept concrete steps to the small, palm-potted foyer and the balding, fastidious clerk behind the cubbyhole counter. Oh yes, Dr. Jones, he said, he would ring Dr. Jones. He did hope Dr. Jones was awake. It was early for Dr. Jones.

And then: Dr. Jones would be down in a few minutes. The morning newspaper was on the table, and magazines, if the gentleman cared for them.

He waited ten minutes and was thinking of asking the clerk to ring again, when a tall, gaunt man in his mid-thirties with a well-barbered goatee walked toward them, wearing an expensive satin robe and matching satin slippers.

"You inquired for me?" he asked. His sharp blue eyes were sunken in a long, compressed face. He stood erect and in spite of his hungry look made an imposing appearance.

Greg rose. "Yes. I'm with the police. My name's Evans."

The scientist offered a soft, warm handshake. "How do you do, Mr. Evans. Perhaps we might sit by the window here."

He led the way. "I heard the news over the radio a few minutes ago. About Jan. It gave me quite a shock. I presume that is why you are here?"

"Yes, it is, Doctor. We always check into these drownings—as a matter of routine. We have no evidence it's anything else. The newspapers—well, you know how they are."

The scientist nodded, fitting a cigarette into an ivory holder. "I doubt if I can be of any assistance, Mr. Evans. I hadn't known Jan long. Let me see now—it was June I began my work here. I'm with the university, you know, on a confidential project."

He smiled pleasantly. "You may think," he continued, indicating his robe, "that I keep strange hours, and I do. I work mostly nights. I find I can do my best thinking then."

"You were saying, Doctor——"

"Oh yes, I met Jan about two weeks after I arrived from London——"

"You're English then, Doctor?"

"By birth, yes, although I have lived so many years in this country that I think of myself as an American. I was with the Manhattan Project during the war. Manhattan, you know, was responsible for the co-ordination of the scientific thought that went into the development of the atomic bomb. Pardon me for digressing. It is most unscientific."

He tapped the ashes precisely into a tray. "I was thinking at the time of buying a home—and bringing my sister and her family over. I believe it was about the last of June that I dropped into the Buller office and Jan showed me about. Our friendship began that day and we saw quite a bit of each other until——"

"I understand," Greg said. He waited a moment. "When did you see her last, Doctor?"

"Saturday night. We went to the wrestling matches—to see Panther Wilson. He was a friend of hers, you know. We always took in his matches."

"May I ask a personal question?"

"Please do. I appreciate your position fully."

"Were you in love with Miss Logan?"

He stared out the window. "I—I don't think so. I am quite certain she did not care for me—in that way. She was a brilliant woman, very attractive, of course, and a wonderful conversationalist. I appreciated that, because this has become a monosyllabic world. We have almost lost the talent for communicating any thoughts except the most concrete. I would say we are gradually retrograding to the primitive in our speech. There I go, digressing again. Pardon me."

"How did she feel about Mr. Wilson?"

He smiled. "You detectives! You think only love breeds violence and death. No, Panther Wilson was a friend, nothing more, like myself. To be frank with you"—he turned to look at Greg—"I doubt if Jan was capable of a deep and lasting love for any man."

"How do you mean that?"

"I dislike saying this, because we were good friends, very good friends. But friends often are friends because they understand and sympathize with each other's faults. It was evident, Mr. Evans, to anyone with a scientific background that Jan was suffering from a deep-seated neurosis. She had a compelling urge to demonstrate her power over men. She felt she had to prove she was a desirable woman."

He took a deep, resigned breath. "You might put me down as the last circumstantial evidence she gathered—and at the best, highly circumstantial evidence."

Greg pursued the subject, finding it intriguing but unproductive. The questioning developed that Dr. Jones knew little about Jan's friends other than Panther Wilson. She had introduced him once to Bill Buller, her employer, and he recalled he had heard her mention Hoagy Anderson. He had no suggestion about Cokie's whereabouts.

He walked Greg to the door. "I won't be attending the funeral. I want to remember Jan—always—as she was."

He offered his hand in good-by, too overcome to speak, and turned back.

As Greg drove away, his mind automatically sorted out the facts and the intangibles, and attempted to file them in neat, systematic order. The only trouble was that facts were mulish and intangibles more so, and often they strayed from their corrals.

One now was balking. He struggled to remember bits of conversation about the Manhattan Project he had heard in the Army. He was under the impression that Manhattan, because of its highly secret work on the atom bomb, had employed only American scientists.

He stopped by home for his wallet, which he had forgotten in his haste that morning. Timmy, a five-year-old redhead from two houses down, rolled up on his scooter. "Can I play with Adam?" he asked.

"Please, Timmy, I've told you. It's Mr. Adam. Let's be respectful."

"Can I play with Mr. Adam?"

"You can if you can find him."

As Timmy went scooting away, Greg heard a screen door slam. Cyn came running down the steps toward him.

"Sweet little monster," he said.

"Isn't he?" she agreed. "I'm going to have six of 'em—three boys and three girls."

She had her life all planned—auto trips on Saturdays, church on Sundays, and a modern house with lots of glass and a fireplace in the dead center of the living room to stumble over.

"All monsters?" Greg asked.

"I hope so. I don't like the quiet ones. Here"—she offered a five-dollar bill—"I made them come across."

The money stopped him in his walk toward the house. A downtown store had overcharged him five dollars. He would have let it ride. But when he mentioned it to Cyn, she had asked for the sales ticket. "You need looking after," she had said.

He now asked curiously, "How'd you explain it to the store? I mean—that you went in for me?"

"I told them I was practicing to become a wife," she answered blithely.

He hesitantly took the five. She added, "Two balcony seats to the *Song of Norway* would cost exactly four-eighty, leaving twenty cents for gas."

"It's a date," he said, laughing.

"Thanks for asking," she tossed back as she hurried for her car.

In the house he telephoned the office and was switched to Homicide. One of the younger detectives answered. "Yeah, we've been trying to reach you all over. A man's confessed to killing Jan Logan. We're holding him in the number two room."

CHAPTER 16

They climbed slowly to Lake Mary, driving through a murky forest that here and there re-flashed the sun's gold from leaves that already were thinking in russet terms of winter. Once they stopped to pick a delicate blue wild flower spun in filigree.

The day was like the flower, but it seldom broke through the trance that held her in bound. A little after three she had awakened screaming, with the man's hands on her in her dream, crushing, stifling her.

And then about dawn, something inside had shaken her roughly and she had aroused with an alarm of a different kind. Until after sunup she lay thinking about little things that were made more frightening by their very nagging. She recognized the worries for what they were—primitive, built-in fears lifted from her psychology textbooks. Everyone on a vacation had them, wondering if his home had burned while he was gone, if his dog died.

It was ridiculous.

Gale broke in on her thoughts. "I still think you should have reported that fiend to someone."

"Maybe so—but it would've just held us up." Every time she

thought of the incident, the fear flushed through her, filling her lungs until she could scarcely breathe. "And I did tell the man at the lodge——"

"He didn't hear a word you said. Hotel people are all like that. They got an automatic built-in head nodder. You can bet he's not going to report it—bad for business."

On a whim, Gale had insisted on quitting Little Bear. "Too quiet," she had said, meaning she hadn't found any interesting fellows. Hastily she and Cokie had written post cards home, saying they were moving on.

They caught a teasing glimpse of Lake Mary as they rounded the last bend, and then as they drew into the clearing before the lodge it spread before them—an oval of turquoise with the sun lying hot and bright on it.

They drove far past the lodge before they found a place to pull in under the trees. Another car moved in alongside them, so close that Cokie was unable to open her door. The man apologized and Cokie said that was all right, she would use the other door. She felt his eyes on her as she slid across the seat and knew they followed her as she walked away from the car. She had barely noticed him, except that he was an older man in need of a shave and haircut.

He called after them, "Can you tell me where the lodge is, girls?"

Gale shot an odd look at Cokie. He had just driven past the lodge; he surely had seen it. "You passed it," Gale said, and walked faster.

At the registration desk a harried clerk was turning others ahead of them away. He was sorry, very sorry, but there were no cottages, no rooms, and no tents. No, he hadn't the slightest idea where they could find accommodations. It was the worst he had seen in ten years. Was there any mail? He didn't know. He would see. If he lived through this, he was going to take an easy job with a road gang.

Cokie recognized Mick's writing as he handed her the letter. Her heart sank. Mick couldn't meet them as he had planned. He had a chance to work in the harvest fields after finishing at the logging camp. He probably would be late for registration at the university.

They stopped in the restaurant to order coffee and talk over the situation. They counted their money, divided it by the number of days left, and came to the conclusion they could afford the Three C Dude Ranch, which was well down the mountain and usually deserted at this time of the year because of the heat.

They went for a swim in the lake then, changing in the public bathhouse. Once in the water, Cokie set out on her course with easy, graceful strokes, moving away from the crowd. Her right hip, which had pained her most of the night, limbered up under the therapy of movement and the warmth of the water.

She thought Gale was following, until she glanced back and saw she had struck up a conversation with three young fellows.

She stroked only enough to keep moving, and soon the night's fears were sliding past her. She remembered another day like this, swimming with her father, and afterward leaning her head against his big frame on the beach, talking. He always had taken to the water to think his way through the harshness of the day, and taken Jan and her with him. He had called them his water puppies, and Jan even more than she had taken to the surf with all the playful zest of a seal.

A water bird took off with a scolding squawk. She realized she had been gone for some time and turned back. Gale was waiting for her, already dressed. "Just a bunch of goofs," she said, dismissing the fellows. "I knew this perfume wouldn't pull in anything I wanted."

At the car she said hurriedly, "I'll drive." Honestly, the way that Cokie drove. She was likely as not to dream right off the road.

They had driven a mile beyond the lodge and were nearing the turnoff for the ranch, when they pulled into a long line of cars barely moving.

Gale stretched her neck. "It's a road block," she said disgustedly. She looked again and reported back, "It's the highway patrol.

Golly, Cokie, I bet it's a checkup—and our brakes! If we have to get new brakes we're broke."

They idled along. The officers looked trim in their tans and businesslike in the holsters slung about their hips. Gale fumed and kept braking the car in short jerky stops. She let out a little gasp of joy then and, before Cokie realized what was happening, gunned the motor and swung the car recklessly into a logging trail. She took the narrow, rutted, bumpy road so fast and wildly she almost lost control. The trail plunged deeper into the forest and then turned, running parallel to the highway. The car bounced high as it hit the potholes and careened dangerously close to trees as it took the turns.

"That's what a college education does for you," Gale said, "and I'm only a sophomore."

CHAPTER 17

At Homicide, Greg conferred briefly outside the number two room with the young detective.

"His name's Benjamin Zee Moore," the detective said hurriedly, referring to a card. "He's an architect, forty-four, lives at 1982 East Thirteenth street."

"What does he say?" Greg asked. The name seemed faintly familiar.

"Nothing, except when he came in he said he'd killed her. My partner and I have been hammering away, but he keeps saying he won't talk to anybody except you."

Greg pushed through the door. Moore came out of his seat, and the other detective put a hand on him. "You did come, you did come," Moore said jubilantly. "I was afraid you wouldn't." He was slight and studious-looking, with intense eyes.

Greg stalled. He had seen the face, but where? A thousand names, a thousand faces slipped in and out every year.

Moore hurried on, a man with a hysteria to talk, "I killed her, I killed her. Her throat was so white and she was so beautiful. I don't know what came over me. Her throat—I felt it and it was so soft and white . . ."

Greg remembered then. "Her throat was so white." It had been four years ago. The Schmerler case.

"Thank you, Mr. Moore, for coming in," he said evenly. "You go home now, and if we need you we'll call you."

Moore looked up at him in shock. "Why, you—you can't do this. I killed her—all by myself. There wasn't anyone else. You think there was someone else."

"If we need you we'll call you," Greg repeated.

Moore shot to his feet. "No, you don't," he shouted. "You did this once before to me. You're not going to do it again."

Greg took him by the arm, walked him to the door, then down the corridor and outside. He was shouting, "Please, you've got to listen. Her throat——"

McTamish of the *News* passed them. "What a police department," he said. "Doesn't even want 'em when they confess."

"I couldn't help it. She lay in my arms. I held her a long time."

Greg indicated to the officer on duty to keep him out. Moore's words trailed after him as he returned to Homicide: "She was so beautiful. Her throat . . ."

Greg told the young Homicide detective, "We wasted a couple of days on the Schmerler case before we found he was a psycho."

Greg picked up a folder from Bill Akers' desk marked: ATTENTION—EVANS. Inside were two teletypes from the FBI in answer to police queries. The first referred to Zump, the unidentified highjacker who was selling Hoagy the $400,000. The teletype read: CHECK FOR NAME ZUMP NEGATIVE.

The other concerned the police request for a criminal record, if any, on Hoagy. It read: EDWARD OSTEN ANDERSON, BORN APRIL 27, 1905, DODGE CITY, KANSAS, SIX FIVE, TWO THIRTY, HAIR DARK BROWN, EYES BROWN, COMPLEXION RUDDY, OCCUPATION AT TIME OF ARREST, BROKERAGE MAN, SCARS OUTER ELBOW, BASE LEFT INDEX FINGER. CRIMINAL RECORD: ARRESTED JAN. 4, 1946, COLUMBUS, OHIO,

SUSPICION MURDER. CHARGES DROPPED FOR LACK OF EVIDENCE JAN. 24, 1946.

Akers had scrawled across the bottom: "Request Columbus forward details."

The file included a couple of memos from Homicide men. One disclosed that Mick Foster, one-time boy friend of Jan Logan and current boy friend of Cokie Logan, had been traced to a logging camp at Timberlake. He had left camp, presumably to return to the university. His present whereabouts were unknown.

The other memo reported that the "mail cover" placed at the post office on the names of Jan Logan and Cokie Logan had produced a post card signed Cokie Logan and postmarked Little Bear two days previously, three bills, four circulars, and several magazines.

A scribbled note from Akers disclosed, moreover, that Gale Roberts' mother had telephoned to report she had received a couple of letters from her daughter. Each said the two were leaving that particular spot and would let her know later where they would be.

He had expected a report on George Pierson, his assailant in Ellen Marshall's apartment, but the officers running down the lead had not called in.

Joe Packer came by then to advise he had finished checking Hoagy Anderson's bank account. "As near as I can tell—from his deposits at the time of the deals—he's getting only a fifteen-percent cut of the profit."

"Well, I'll be," Greg said.

"It's something to think about," Packer added.

Packer was right. It was something to think about. If Malone was taking eighty-five per cent . . .

On the way out, Greg studied the surveillance chart nailed to the wall by the door. Only occasional spot checks—instead of a round-the-clock watch—were being run on Hoagy Anderson, Bill Buller, the realtor, Panther Wilson, the wrestler, and Dr. C. Oxford Jones, the scientist. He could hear Bill Akers say gruffly, "The taxpayers get what they pay for."

CHAPTER 18

Greg knew he had surprised George Benson dozing. A girl on Tech 9 was saying, ". . . every time I walk into a knitting shop I wish I was an octopus so I could knit a dozen dresses at the same time," and over Tech 7 came, ". . . you add two tablespoons of sugar and a half cup of flour and then you mix."

"It's a college education," George said. He reported that Joan, the little girl with polio, now had a fighting chance.

Greg said, "Good," and realized how weak a word was compared to a man's feeling.

"Panther Wilson did some talking. I cut the tape and put it on your desk. Hoagy will talk to Malone in a few minutes. He called Malone about an hour ago, but Malone couldn't talk. The doctor was with his mother. They think she has a broken hip."

"Be sure to call me, George."

In his office Greg played all the tapes back, listening intently. A conviction was growing that the words that spilled out of the talking bugs might eventually break Malmo, might even find Cokie Logan. It might not be in what they said. It might be in what they didn't say. It might be in what they tried to cover up. It might even be in the pauses that sometimes told more than the words themselves.

Panther Wilson talked with an unidentified man. The log showed the call had been placed at 11:31 A.M.

"Hello."

"Nicky? This is your old friend, Panther."

"Hello, Panther. What's new?"

"I got me some panther trunks—real, honest panther fur."

"That I've got to see. Say, Panther, Betty's still talking about you playing clown for the kids at the hospital."

"I got a bigger kick out of it than the kids. Say, I called to tell you a copper was around asking about Jan."

"What did he want to know?"

"I told him to get the hell out."

The pause was noticeable, and then, "You shouldn't have done that, Panther."

"Why not? The way I figure, if they got something on you, they'll pick you up. If they haven't, they can't. Why treat the bastards nice?"

"I never knew you were a cop hater."

"Ha!" Everything in the room trembled as the laugh boomed in the playback. "He wanted to know where the kid sister was. And me with a post card in my pocket all the time."

"Are you worried?"

"Nah. How's Betty?"

"She's going to have a baby."

"You mean it?"

"I sure do."

"Well, tell her I hope it doesn't look like you."

The rest of the conversation was mostly banter. It ended with Panther promising to leave two tickets to the matches at the box office. It was a lead that Homicide might like to follow.

After hastily scanning the morning's output of typed transcripts on the other techs and finding nothing pertinent, Greg returned to the Tech Room. He pulled a straight chair alongside 66.

George said, "I thought you might like to get your friend to autograph this." He handed him a newspaper picture of Panther. Greg laughed and tossed it in the wastebasket.

The dialing began then, quick and definite. It came over two playbacks, Tech 66 on Malone and the new Tech, 22, on Hoagy. To avoid confusion, they shut off 22.

"I've got a couple of things, Blitz."

"Very well."

"One of the boys from the police department was around asking about the girl. Name of Evans."

"Why would he talk with you?"

"Don't worry, Blitz, it's all right. They're seeing everyone who knew her. I used to have a few drinks with her, dated her a few times. I was glad he came around. Gave me a chance to get myself on record."

"That's all right."

"I don't make as many mistakes as you think, Blitz."

"You never make a mistake—when you think."

"One more thing—the police know she was bumped off."

"I had expected that."

"The papers said an informant told them."

"How could anyone know?"

"Nobody could. It's just newspaper talk. McTamish may have the lowdown on his broadcast tonight."

"Have you heard from them?"

Hoagy's hesitation was marked. He said slowly then, "They lost her, but they know someone who knows where she is."

Greg turned back to his office as the click of the receivers came over. He had been sitting lost in thought for a few minutes when the phone rang. Termie, the bug man, called to report he had traced the lead wire—on the microphone they had found in Ellen Marshall's living room—to an apartment house two doors away.

"The apartment's rented in the name of the guy you slugged," he said. "George Pierson. He took it a month ago—on a year's lease. I ran a trace on Pierson."

Greg said, "Yes?" and Termie continued, "He's a private dick —with offices in the Wacker Building. Two one eight. His client's Harry Malone."

"How do you know?"

Termie laughed, and Greg did not pursue the point. He knew Termie had cut in on Pierson's telephone line—without asking Lancaster's permission. He could tap a line by induction, without actually hooking into it, and the tap would set up such little interference that no one would suspect it.

"Pierson's got one of those new deals on the bug," Termie continued. "An automatic tape recorder. He has to come in only once a day to change the tape."

Almost the second he hung up, the phone rang again. The switchboard at headquarters was transferring a call. A man's voice came over. He was the hotel clerk who had summoned Dr. Jones that morning.

"Oh, Mr. Evans," he said in a high, breaking voice. "I don't know whether I should be doing this—not at all. I may lose my position if the manager should ever——"

Greg interrupted. "No one's going to know. I'll see to that."

"Thank you—I could tell you were a man of your word. It is about Dr. C. Oxford Jones—the scientist—you talked with him in the foyer."

"What about Dr. Jones?"

"The most curious thing happened. He went upstairs after you left, and a half hour passed, and he came down and said he was leaving—leaving for good. He was already packed, and when I asked where I should forward his mail he gave me a peculiar stare. A most peculiar stare, and said he would let me know.

"On my lunch hour—I really shouldn't have—but I only had an egg sandwich because Ruth—that's my wife—didn't get up in time. Well, on my lunch hour I took the stairs—I didn't want the elevator boy to know—and went to his room, and everything was in a dither of a state, if I might say so. A dither of a state."

Greg asked questions. Did Dr. Jones have much luggage? He had three suitcases and a steamer trunk. Did he call a moving company? No, he took a taxi. How long had Dr. Jones lived there? And so on.

When he finished he placed a call to Homicide. He learned that while an occasional spot surveillance had been run on Dr. Jones the day before, the men had been pulled off for a murder that had broken that morning, a knifing on the East Side.

He talked next with university officials, who advised him Dr. Jones had been employed the previous June 1 as a nuclear physicist on peacetime atomic use. The job was neither as secret nor as important as he had made out, but then almost every man did that. In an industrialized, urbanized age, a man had to justify his importance to escape the feeling he was a statistic on a pay roll.

95

His associates thought well of him, both as a man and a scientist. His background included degrees from Edinburgh.

At Greg's request Personnel agreed to forward a photograph of Dr. Jones that was attached to his record, as well as a copy of the record.

CHAPTER 19

They made their way slowly through the dusky gym, toward the one hot bright light in the place, an arc that shot a white spot straight down on the four-poster ring. The row on row of empty seats painted white gave the place a cemetery feeling.

Greg's arms swung easily; Packer chewed his gum a little harder.

Panther in trunks slipped into a robe by ringside and turned and saw them. His eyes stayed with them. They came up on each side, making a triangle. He was breathing heavily, having just climbed down from the mat after the afternoon workout.

A silence, as if on cue, fell over the other wrestler and the hangers-on. Greg said quietly, "Panther, I want you to meet Joe Packer. He's working with me."

Panther shot Joe a quick glance and as quickly relegated him to the background.

"He has some questions."

"Could we sit down?" Packer asked. "It won't take long."

"Shortstop!" Panther yelled, and a little gray-haired man materialized. "Shortstop," said Panther, "my nerves are going to be too shot to work tonight—unless I get a little privacy."

"Don't flip, Panther—for goodness sake don't flip." Shortstop appealed to Packer. "Please, mister, will you leave?"

Packer argued furiously. He was a good actor and turned in such a diverting performance that Greg eased away without Panther noticing.

Losing himself quickly in the dusk, he took a short cut across a row of empty seats. He counted the doors as he walked down the shadowy corridor, which was brought barely alive by one naked bulb.

In a matter of seconds he was inside Panther's dressing room, closing the door softly behind him. Using a pencil flashlight, he took quick stock of the cubbyhole. Panther's clothes, arranged neatly on a hanger, hung by a cracked shaving mirror. His hand went into the inside coat pocket and brought out a packet of envelopes and papers with a rubber band around them. As he sorted through the contents the post card fell to the floor. In the pencil light he noted the postmark of Lake Mary and read: "Hi, Panther—We're having loads of fun but can't get a room here. Going to the Three C. Have fun. Cokie."

Returning the packet to the inside pocket, he heard a shuffling in the corridor and snapped off the flashlight. A light came on overhead and Beer Barrel stood in the doorway.

"Excuse me," Greg said, and shoved past him. He covered the corridor in a few long strides, Beer Barrel trailing. As he came up to Packer, who was still arguing, he said, "Joe, forget it. You're wrecking the man's nerves."

As they walked away, Greg glanced back. Panther was looking after them. His face said he was being tricked. He didn't know how, and he didn't like it.

CHAPTER 20

From her chair on the porch, Gale followed the red sun ball down. The long twilight, with a hot, dry, spiced breeze coming in from the east, had begun some minutes before. She rose to look anxiously toward the corral where a wrangler was helping a man dismount. Darn that Cokie, riding off by herself.

97

She saw the ranchwoman hustling toward her, all two hundred pounds and five feet of her. She came up breathless. "Miss Logan's wanted on the phone."

"She's out riding," Gale said. "She should've been back before this."

The ranchwoman said, "Thank you, hon," and hurried away.

It's Jan, Gale thought. She sauntered toward the corral. The afternoon riders were beginning to drift in. She recognized the Abercrombies as they swung down from their horses, stiff-legged, and walked painfully toward her.

She heard her name being shouted and waved to let the ranchwoman know she was coming. She took boyish strides, her shirt billowing out over her levis.

"Hon," the ranchwoman said from the top of the steps, "they want to talk with you since Miss Logan isn't about."

The phone was on the wall, almost too high for her. She picked up the receiver and a man asked in a clipped, hurried manner, "Miss Gale Roberts?"

"Yes?"

He identified himself, and her heart quickened at the word "police."

"I have some bad news," he said. "Jan Logan was drowned Monday night. Her body was washed up at Sandy Beach."

She said something, she never knew what. He hurried on, but it couldn't be, what he was saying. It simply couldn't be. She sagged against the wall, her head throbbing, her throat dry.

He asked if she understood and she answered, yes. Cokie was in some kind of danger. She and Cokie were to stay in the main room of the lodge until officers arrived. They were to talk with no one, go no place, no matter who asked or what the circumstances might be.

He was saying good-by, and it wasn't until he was gone that she realized she hadn't told him about Cokie. She was running wildly out the door, down the steps, stumbling, picking herself up, racing across the graveled courtyard.

The wrangler was uncinching a pinto mare. "Could you saddle a horse for me?" she asked.

"It's getting late, miss," he said.

"My friend—something terrible has happened. Please—will you come with me?"

He shrugged and began cinching the pinto back up. These young'uns thought they had troubles too.

She waited impatiently, straining her eyes to follow the trail through the dusk. And then she saw Cokie riding over the brow of a hill, all alone, riding toward her.

CHAPTER 21

Joe Packer was coming out of the kitchen of the Malmo apartment when Greg arrived. Packer was in his shirt sleeves, with his collar open and tie pulled askew. He was sipping a cup of steaming coffee with a hand none too steady.

"Care for some java?"

"Not now."

"Well," said Packer, raising the cup perilously in the air, "here's to another kill by Old 66." Some of the coffee spilled over.

"What's new?" Greg asked, indicating the "window," which was blacked out.

"Nothing. She came in half an hour ago with packages and disappeared into the back of the apartment." He held his watch to his ear to satisfy himself it was ticking. "Ten minutes to show time," he remarked, and added, "I hope it's better than the last O.W. duty I drew. The couple sat around and discussed Ma Fen half the night. You common people, of course," he continued, smiling, "probably don't know who Ma Fen was. That's the trouble with the world—ignorance."

The "window" lighted up and they walked over to watch. Ellen

99

Marshall was wearing tight black satin hostess pants and a simple white blouse. She went to the phonograph cabinet and chose the records thoughtfully, occasionally rejecting one she had already selected.

The music vibrated painfully against their eardrums until Greg turned the playback volume down. "You would have to plant a bug next to the record player," Packer said.

She briefly inspected her hair and make-up before the mirror. Greg imagined he could almost hear her breathing. Her lips, as she touched them, were but a few inches away. They fell at the corners, giving her a downbeat expression that vanished when she was animated. It's that way with many women, he thought; they are beautiful only in movement.

She read, idly turning the pages, studying fashion pictures, until Malone arrived. Packer picked up the log and wrote, "Malone entered Marshall apartment, 11:41 P.M."

"I'm glad you got over, Blitz," she whispered, kissing him.

"I can stay only a little while." She took his hat, placed it on a table, and sat by him on the divan, taking his hand in hers.

"How is your mother?" she asked.

"Not so good. She's suffering quite a bit. At her age—I'm worried, Marsh."

She held a match for his cigarette. "I wish I could come over."

He reacted quickly. "You know how she feels . . ."

"Go ahead," she said bitterly. "Finish the sentence. How she feels—about me."

"Please, Marsh. Not tonight."

She rose and, going to the opposite wall, pulled out a rectangular panel that revealed a bar. As she mixed the drinks his eyes stayed with her. "I've never seen a woman who could be so fully dressed and look so naked."

She brought him his glass, pleased. "You haven't said anything like that in ages."

"I might add I've never known anyone to mix a better martini." He settled back comfortably. "I talked with Hoagy today."

Greg signaled the cameraman, and in the Malmo apartment the whir of film passing through sprockets came over.

"Good old Hoagy," she whispered. She had her arm around his neck, her head on his shoulder.

"He mentioned a man called Zump. I couldn't place him."

"Zump! Why, darling, you know him. The Priest!"

"Ah-h." His eyes lighted up. "I know the Priest, of course. He was with us on the Venezuela deal. If Hoagy had called him the Priest—I would have known."

"I wish we were back in Chicago," she said dreamily. "It was fun."

Malone's tone changed abruptly. "I've told you, Marsh, and I'm going to be firm about it. I never want you to mention Chicago." It was an old irritant, a scab she had raked. He continued, "I've tried to explain to you. I've been patient about it."

She waggled her head saucily. "You want everyone to think you've always been a success. You won't even talk about the old days." She laughed low. "I can remember when you stuffed cardboard in your shoes——"

"Marsh! I told you. I meant it." The anger came through.

She got up to find a cigarette. "I know. We're somebody now, aren't we?"

"I didn't mean that. You know it."

"You're somebody. A big shot on The Row. But I'm not." She hesitated, and then said slowly, "I haven't a thing I can call my own."

He moved to the edge of the divan. "There isn't anything you can't have. You know that."

"What about the Cadillac——"

"I told you. People would talk about you."

"Oh yes—and there's the five thousand dollars . . ." She trailed off. "There's a spastic home for children around the corner. I want a thousand dollars for it, Blitz."

He stood up. "What are you thinking about? I can't afford that kind of money. I've told you——"

"You lost two thousand dollars in a poker game last month. You told me so yourself."

Malone shrugged and sat back down. "Maybe you should go back to Chicago, Marsh, and pick up the old life. You've never been happy here."

She stood quiet for a moment, studying him. "If you don't want me, say so."

He made no answer. "Want another?" she asked, pouring herself a drink. He shook his head.

"You feel loyal to me, don't you?" she continued. "That's all it is. Like I'm your aunt or something."

He was cool. "Maybe it'd be better for both of us, Marsh."

She screamed, "You're never going to put me out to pasture."

"Marsh, please! People can hear you."

"I don't care," she said weakly, falling to the divan. He glanced at his watch. "Do you mind?" he asked, going to the radio. He tuned in McTamish's midnight news broadcast. She sat quietly, toying with a handkerchief, never once looking up.

The broadcast over, she turned off the radio. "I'm sorry, darling," she said. "I—I get such a caged feeling—shut up here."

"I know, Marsh."

"But honestly, Blitz, what good's your money doing you?"

He took a long breath. "It's something, Marsh—I can't understand it myself. I went hungry as a boy. I swore if I ever got any money . . ."

He pulled her to him. "Marsh, it doesn't make sense. I know it doesn't. But I've always had a dread of ending up on Madison—in a flophouse."

She looked at him sharply for a moment, and finally a slow smile came into her eyes. Then she took his head in her hands and kissed him gently. His arms tightened about her until she gasped, "Blitz, you're hurting me."

She tried to tease him into staying, but he left shortly afterward. As she came back from the door her face lost its life. She stubbed out her cigarette with a hard twist, turned the lights off, and left the room.

"Not bad," Greg said, turning away from the window with Packer. "I hadn't hoped for this much."

He referred to his notes. "We know Zump is also called the Priest and that Malone is tight with his money. Malone would like to rid himself of Ellen Marshall; she knows it and is panicky about it. She probably realizes that her old weapon, sex, has lost its magnetic draw. She has a feud on with his mother, or perhaps it's the other way around."

They knew, too, the kind of cigarette he smoked, the drink he liked, and that he apparently tuned in regularly on McTamish's news broadcast.

Before they left the apartment, Greg placed a call to Homicide. A detective on graveyard answered laconically to let him know he had interrupted a poker session. The detective reported the highway patrol had brought Miss Cokie Logan and Miss Gale Roberts to headquarters, and they had been questioned for two hours. Homicide then had sent the two by police car to Miss Logan's apartment. Miss Roberts had agreed to spend the night with her. Homicide, moreover, had assigned officers and detectives to stake the apartment.

A transcript of the questions and answers would be available by 9 A.M. tomorrow if Greg cared to read it. The detective didn't think he would find much. Miss Logan had no idea, he reported, why anyone would have slain her sister or would plot to do away with her.

"But she's okay," he said. He meant he didn't think she was holding back.

CHAPTER 22

The next morning he dragged out of bed when the alarm went off at seven. He showered, fed Mr. Adam, and took five minutes to sip coffee boiling hot, reading the *News* as he did so.

He found a by-line piece by McTamish engrossing. McTamish had a knack for making a commonplace story graphic, a talent no one would suspect in talking with the man.

Before leaving the house he called the Tech Room. Old 66 had been quiet for almost twenty-four hours.

Even at this time of morning he felt the sweat on him as he drove to the apartment building where Cokie Logan lived. He thought of his first trip there, that day he had come groping, seeking to identify a nameless woman found on a beach.

As he parked he spotted the radio car on the side street and another across from the entrance. He heard, too, a door open a crack as he went down the second-floor corridor to her apartment, and knew a Homicide man was checking. The newspapers would say she was being afforded "maximum police protection," and the stereotyped phrase would carry assurance to everyone—except the police. Every detective on the stake-out this day would be remembering that in the Dragona extortion the key witness had been shot in his sleep with three officers on guard outside his house, and in the Hutchins' gangland case the suspect himself had been slain inside a police cordon. Always there was an opening sometime, a minute or two when a slayer, if he were ready, could take the life he had been stalking.

Still, Greg thought, the police held the odds. The opening might be there, but the escape route could be fraught with danger. It was a slow, tedious, maddening hunt for the murderer, who must wait for that split second when every circumstance was favorable, and seize it, and not err. Few killers had the patience or the judgment or the decisiveness.

He heard a rustle inside after knocking, and Gale Roberts opened the door. "I'm Greg Evans—with the police," he said.

"Do you have to? She's so broken up."

"I'm sorry," he said, entering. The room was crowded with a couple of university students, an older woman, and Panther Wilson. Greg asked if they would step outside for a few minutes.

Panther put an arm big-brother-like about Cokie, squeezing her. "I got to be going," he said with feeling. "You know the old Panther's around if you want him." He kissed her hair. As he left he avoided Greg's eyes.

Cokie said quietly, "Won't you sit down?" and in that instant he liked her.

She sat in an armchair that almost swallowed her, kicked off her shoes, and pulled her legs under. He pushed a panda to one side as he took the divan. Gale moved toward the door. "If it's all right, I'll run out for a pack of cigarettes." She added, "I'm staying with Cokie a few days."

The room was a blend of soft pastels and uncluttered modern with Hawaiian prints on the blue walls and fussy lamps about. A couple of traveling bags, opened, were in a corner where they had been dropped the night before. A color photograph of Jan and Cokie, blown up from a snapshot, stood on the cocktail table. It had been taken at least a couple of years before, and Jan had a sweet dark look about her. A couple of years . . .

Cokie gave her hair a toss, and he saw her hands clench. She nodded as if to say, I'm ready.

"I know the officers asked last night if you had any idea—we thought you might this morning."

"No—I tried to think—but nothing came. We—we were very close."

She tightened up all over to hold the tears back. "One of the officers," she said, "he asked horrible questions. . . ."

"We walk into a case, Miss Logan, we know nothing about the people—and in our work the world isn't pretty."

She leaned her head back, closing her eyes. She was breathing with effort.

He continued, "Sometimes relatives are prone to hold things back—but if there is anything——"

Over and over he had seen it happen—good people unwilling to confide a vital fact to the police, preferring to let the guilty go unpunished, often to risk their own lives, rather than expose a skeleton in the closet.

"No," she said. She was far away.

He pressed. "The killer may be counting on you to keep quiet.

Not to tell us right away, at least. But you must remember: if there is anything, he will never feel safe as long as you're around."

She had fire in her eyes. "Jan was the sweetest person . . ."

She looked then out the window at a squirrel scampering around a tree. "There's Monkeyface," she said. "Jan named him."

He made a decision. "I want to ask a question or two in confidence."

She nodded.

"Do you know a man named Harry Malone? He runs a brokerage house."

She looked at him curiously. "No," she said after a second of thought.

"Ellen Marshall?" Again the shake of the head. "Or Ed Anderson? He has a nickname—Hoagy."

"Should I know them?" she asked.

"I thought your sister might have mentioned them."

"I don't think so."

He inquired then concerning the whereabouts of Mick Foster, her boy friend, and she repeated what she had told the officers the night before, that she expected him shortly. He asked if she thought she would hear from Dr. Jones, the scientist—she hadn't yet been told he had disappeared—and she answered that she would, since he was Jan's closest friend.

"They were practically engaged," she said.

He retraced another path the Homicide officers had taken—the habit patterns of her sister, exploring in detail Jan's custom of walking to the beach two and three evenings a week, about an hour before sundown, and returning at dusk so she would be ahead of the dark.

"She hadn't been herself for a week or so," she said. She tried to clear the grief from her throat. "She was awfully upset about something. I don't know what."

"Perhaps if you went back over each day . . . Could you try?"

Dr. Jones, she said, had come in for dinner Sunday. She and her sister had gone to the beach Saturday. The Wednesday before they had seen a Vic Mature movie.

"Oh," she said, startled by a remembrance.

"Yes?"

She said Friday a week ago they went to an Italian restaurant, the Capri, to celebrate a sale Jan had made, and Jan was so disturbed she scarcely knew where she was. When Cokie asked her about it, she had brushed it off as "nerves."

"The day before—it was her birthday. She was all right then. I made a cake—the icing ran. . . ."

Greg rose, a good feeling inside, the kind he had on discovering a fact that might work into something. "Thanks a lot," he said.

She came with him to the door in her shoeless feet. "You've been awfully kind," she said.

He stopped downstairs at the manager's apartment. Julia Bunker met him in the same blue shorts and matching halter.

"May I talk with you a minute?" he asked.

"Come in," she said blithely. "The name's Evans, isn't it?"

She sat across from him, entwining long legs that had never been exposed to the sun. The halter swayed uncertainly as she bent to fix a shoelace.

"I'm sorry about the other night at Mac's," she said.

"You needn't be."

"I'm going to give up Mac's for Lent."

"That's a long time away."

"All my good resolutions are—but somebody said—I can't remember who—that as long as you have resolutions, even if they are far away . . ." She laughed. "May I get you a drink?"

"No, thanks."

"Don't you love that Cokie? She's strictly from Shelley and Browning. I was, too, once." She turned morose. "Maybe it's too bad we don't all die young."

"Un-huh. I wanted to say we hate to bother you like this—with detectives all over the place——"

"You're not bothering me. Any time *you* want anything, *you* ask me."

"Thanks."

"Is it agreed, then, that *you* do the asking? I don't like to have strange men coming up to my door. Those officers this morning—they gave me the creeps."

"All right, Miss Bunker." He moved toward the door. "And thanks for letting us use the apartment across the way from Cokie's."

As he got into his car, he thought how time now rode with the killer. Lancaster would begin pulling men off in a few days—the next time a murder broke and he needed them. In a city of two million, Lancaster couldn't provide guard service for every person threatened with death.

CHAPTER 23

He met McTamish as he entered the *News*. McTamish stopped to pass the time of day, and Greg could almost see the wheels spinning. McTamish thought he was visiting the *News* to complain to the city editor, and Greg enjoyed letting him think just that.

At the counter he asked the boy for the file copy of the current month. He turned the pages until he reached the Friday he wanted. The headline leaped out at him: BANK MESSENGER KILLED, ROBBED OF $60,000.

The story read:

Mathias P. Black, 63, First National Bank messenger, was shot to death and robbed of $60,000 shortly after 1 P.M. today on the Old Blankenship Road.

His slayer fired three bullets at close range from a .45 revolver. The bullets entered the chest.

He was found dying by Mr. and Mrs. Ben Sack, farmers in the Mission area, who were driving to town. They told sheriff's deputies they remembered a car had passed them shortly before but they were unable to describe it.

Bank officials said Black was taking the $60,000 to Sam's Super-

market in Northport. The market, they said, was in the habit of cashing pay-roll checks Fridays for the workers in the newly built aeronautics plant. Northport has no bank.

Deputies surmised, from the position of Black's body, he had resisted the holdup. He was carrying the money in a locked bag in the trunk of a 1952 sedan. The trunk lock had been shot away.

He read the account several times, thanked the boy, and left. At Homicide he talked with the two detectives assigned the case. They had "checked out" and drawn a "dry run." No clues, no suspects. They had obtained the serial numbers on the bills from the First National Bank, which had recorded them as a part of its routine procedure before turning the money over to the messenger. They had broadsided the serial numbers to every bank in the state and the surrounding six states.

As the detectives reconstructed the slaying, Mathias Black had been stopped by a ruse. Perhaps someone had played dead on the highway or had posed as a road worker and held up a STOP sign. Otherwise Black, who was an experienced messenger, would never have brought his car to a halt. What had happened then was obvious. His assailant—or assailants—had covered him and ordered him out of the car. As he stepped out, he had lunged for one.

A short time later, Greg left headquarters, his thoughts in a whirl.

CHAPTER 24

Everyone had gone, and Gale wondered if Cokie, too, experienced the relief she did. They had said the same phrases, haltingly, not sure of themselves, because what were words at such a time?

She brought the hot chocolate and they sat sipping, with the light fading as the sun moved around the corner of the building.

Cokie said, "I wish Mick would come." She longed so for him, longed to hear him talking in that low, soft way of his, wanting his rough hand on hers.

"I know, Cokie," Gale said. She added, "I'm going home for some clothes—if you think you'll be all right?"

After Gale was gone she broke, unable to stem longer the grief building up in her. In a few minutes it passed and she sat quietly.

The rap startled her. "It's me, Cokie. Bill Buller."

He came in, saying, "I tried to get up sooner, but you know how it is. Golly Moses, I'm all knocked out about this."

He tried to subdue his hearty voice, but a whisper of his would have carried. "It's none of my business, but if the police hadn't tried to cover up, call it a drowning . . ."

"May I take your hat?" she asked by rote. Everything she did was by habit. She heard her own voice, but it seemed it was someone else talking.

"No, I mustn't stay long." He was standing over her, rolling the hat nervously in his hand, looking down in a strange way. She listened for the click of the kitchen-door latch, which would indicate a detective had slipped in to listen. But there was no sound, except the muted ticking of the kitchen clock.

"I don't know if Jan ever said much about me," Bill Buller continued. He walked to the window and looked up and down the street. "You know how it is in business. You have little differences, but they never mean anything. All forgotten the next day."

She looked at him curiously. She never had liked him, because Jan hadn't. She struggled to recall little stories Jan had told, but her memory was blurred.

"Here's a check," he said, taking out a wallet. "It's Jan's commission on that last sale. Figured you might need it."

He added, "I'm going to miss her a lot—both as a friend and a business associate. She was a wonderful person, Cokie, and if anybody says anything about her . . ."

She looked at him questioningly.

"Oh, you know how it is, Cokie. A pretty woman in business. She's sex with a capital S. She's bound to be talked about."

Here it was again, the veiled hint she had heard at headquarters the night before, the snide, prying questions.

"The police——" she began, and stopped.

"Don't let it bother you. They always ask questions. I suppose they're all over the place like termites?"

He waited pointedly. She changed the subject. She might have confided in Panther. He was like a big brother. She remembered now that when Jan had taken the job at the Buller Realty she had returned home furious the first night. Buller had made a pass.

He said, "If there's anything I can do, well, you know you can count on me. I'm as near as the telephone, as they say in the ads— and if you ever need a job, come around."

At the door he turned, "You take care of yourself," and was gone, a strong wind that had blown in and out, almost overpowering.

CHAPTER 25

He was sitting on the front step, having a sandwich, when Cyn drifted over, trailed by Mr. Adam. The late-evening sun, slanting low, burnished her hair.

"Hi," she said, sitting down beside him and spreading out her Mexican skirt. Mr. Adam sat down too.

"How went the autographing?" he asked.

"I'll never marry a man whose name is Johnson," she said.

"Why don't you write Evans for a while?"

"Because Johnson has all the right curlicues. It tests a pen better than any other name."

For a few minutes, as they talked, she lifted him out of the sordidness of the day, away from the chatter of the talking bugs.

But the bugs were on his mind more and more, and he fell to discussing them.

"It's a different kind of society today," he said. "The police have to change their methods—use everything that science can give them. Once a criminal was a lone wolf, but now he works inside syndicates and networks and conspiracies. He uses the telephone to dodge us—so we can't trail him."

"I don't like it, Greg," she said simply. She didn't understand "invasion of privacy," or Supreme Court decisions, or all the legal backgrounds. She added, "I can't help it—it does something to me."

He thought about her answer a moment. It was a feeling, not an analysis. He guessed most people reacted that way. They simply didn't like the sound of it. . . .

En route to the Tech Room, he stopped off at Homicide. Detectives were swarming over the huge, sorry-looking room, all showing the brutal effects of a sweltering day and the fatiguing ravages of working under pressure and speed. At Akers' desk four were checking off possible leads in the disappearance of the scientist, Dr. C. Oxford Jones.

The records of a taxicab company disclosed Dr. Jones had been taken to a downtown hotel at 157 Massachusetts Avenue. But he was not registered there, at least not under the name of C. Oxford Jones. The detectives had compared handwriting samples from his university personnel record with the signatures of the hotel's guests. None matched. They theorized he had checked his luggage and then either walked or taken a streetcar to another destination and returned later for his bags.

A "pick up and hold" had been sent out, and by tomorrow every radio car would be furnished with a copy of his personnel-record photograph.

No one surmised about his guilt. He had established himself as a suspect by his disappearance. It was their job to find him, to question him. As of now, he was a fact on a sheet of paper that had to be disposed of with a negative or a positive after his name. . . .

The Tech Room, since it was now the dinner hour, was cricketing away. ". . . you tell that little snip if I ever catch her . . ."

". . . it closed at 58 . . ."

". . . my innards aren't so good . . . The doctor says I've got to go under the knife . . ."

". . . he doesn't have an inferiority complex, honey . . . he's just plain inferior . . ."

George Benson finished circling the horseshoe, listening a moment to each bug, assuring himself he was missing nothing that might be pertinent. "I think we got something a half hour ago," he said.

He handed Greg a spool of tape. "Hoagy phoned the highjacker," he continued. "He said," and George read from the log, " 'Everything okay?' and Zump answered back, 'Yes,' and they hung up. But I recorded Hoagy dialing the number."

Greg felt a stir go through him as George handed him a slip of paper that had scrawled on it: OX-63728. George had used a machine to record the "pulsations" of Hoagy's dialing. The machine had punched out the "pulsations" on tape. George had then decoded them and come up with the phone number Hoagy had dialed.

"The call went through a switchboard," George continued, "but I couldn't make out what the girl said."

Greg asked then about Joan, and George said, "Her mom thinks if she can pull through another twenty-four hours . . ."

He hesitated. "It's like she was my own," he continued, because a man cooped up in a tech room needed to talk. "Isn't it funny how these folks become real? You hate some of 'em and you love some of 'em and yet you only hear 'em talk."

Greg agreed. Words told a lot, and sometimes even more when they stood out alone, stripped of faces and forms, utterly bodyless. No engaging personalities distracted you, no vivacious sparkle of the eyes or winning smile.

He noticed then the sign George had lettered and hung on the far wall. It read: ZOUNDS! I WAS NEVER SO BETHUMPED WITH WORDS —King John.

Bethumped. That was exactly how he felt.

Miss Cabot came into his office as he sat down. She smiled pleasantly, as usual, as she handed him a stack of typed transcripts. "Anything good?" he asked.

"You'll find a recipe for angel-food cake on Tech 6," she said.

His laugh followed her. From the bottom desk drawer he took a confidential book that listed the phone numbers numerically and then the name of the party and the address. OX-63728 belonged to a downtown hotel, the Meridian.

He was disappointed. It wasn't much of a lead. Zump might be one of eight hundred guests at the hotel or he might not be staying there.

Greg decided he would work the lead out himself, perhaps with Joe Packer. An idea, too daring to admit even to himself, had been wandering aimlessly about the last day. It was an idea that depended on whether he could identify Zump and tail him to the highjacking job and "sit in" on the job itself. It depended, too, on whether he could persuade McTamish into committing a deliberate journalistic sin.

The whole idea appeared unlikely and he thought it was probably only a wishful dream, a plan perfected in the dark of his bed, only to be cracked full of holes next morning at headquarters, by the smells, the montage of faces going by in the dingy halls, the rules, the badges, and the uniforms.

He read transcripts until seven-thirty. The paper work was an enemy that devoured his time, his energy. He would clean up one batch, only to have Miss Cabot bring another. It was an endless business. Not dull nor routine, but endless. A conveyor belt in a factory that moved even in his sleep.

At seven-thirty he returned to the Tech Room. Old 66 had reported earlier that Hoagy would talk with Malone at seven-thirty and that Malone would call for Ellen Marshall later to take her to an unknown place.

Old 66 began pumping at seven thirty-one. Malone expected as sharp punctuality from Hoagy as anyone, although he surely knew that Hoagy was not by nature circumscribed by watch hands.

Greg felt the tension, his and George Benson's. Hoagy began by asking about Malone's mother. Malone was obviously in a hurry. He brushed aside the solicitous remarks and came to the point.

"I've concluded arrangements on the deal," he said.

"Yes, Blitz."

"A messenger from the First National Bank will deliver $100,000 to you at 5 P.M. September 21. It can be in any denomination the Priest wants."

Greg explained, "That's Zump."

Malone continued, "I want you to take the midnight plane out of here that same night——"

"You mean me, personally?"

"Yes, I don't want anyone else. It's too much money."

"I don't know——"

"I'll do the thinking."

"Sure, Blitz, sure."

"You'll take the money to this address in Madrid—126 Santiago Avenue. S-a-n-t-i-a-g-o. Have you got that?"

"One twenty-six Santiago Avenue."

"You'll find a brokerage house there, Cardenas and Sons. You will deliver it to Aleman Cardenas." Again Malone spelled out the names.

"Okay."

"You understand you're to take the midnight plane? In these cases—the other partners—well, they may attempt to recover their investment. The Priest might leave himself open."

"I got you."

"I'll have to go now. Oh." Malone paused. "Did you hear Mc-Tamish last night?"

"Yeah."

"I presume the girl didn't have much to say."

"They don't think so, Blitz. They figure she's too broken up— and doesn't want to show her sister up for what she was."

115

"I take it that ends the matter?"

"No, they're afraid she'll get to thinking about it—when she's over crying—and spill it. They have a plan set for tomorrow night."

"Well, it's none of our business, thank heavens."

"Has that money been—cleared?"

"Yes—definitely."

And with that they said good-by.

George switched off the tape recorder. "Christopher! What a cold fish."

Greg stood in thought, hearing Hoagy's question, "Has that money been—cleared?" It was the first indication over 66 that the murder of Jan Logan and the plotted slaying of Cokie were tied in with serialized money Hoagy and Malone had purchased.

"Yes—definitely," Malone had said. The money had been disposed of, they need not worry. "*It's none of our business, thank heavens.*"

CHAPTER 26

Through the "window" they watched as Ellen Marshall moved nervously about the room. She picked up a newspaper, folded it to an inside page, and propped it up on a table. She lit one cigarette from the stub of another and then viciously crunched out the stub.

"As the Irish would say," commented Joe Packer, "she's in a black mood tonight."

She was at the door almost before they heard the knock.

"Come in," she said.

It was apparent Malone recognized the tone by the feline wariness he showed as he walked in. "I thought we had a date," he said, indicating the negligee.

"I don't feel like going out." She flounced down in a far chair and threw her legs across the arm, letting the negligee fall back.

He started to sit and paused midway as his eyes fell on the paper. "For heaven's sakes, Marsh," he said, raising his voice slightly. "Is that what's disturbing you?"

"I suppose I'm to ignore your piccadilloes?"

"Peccadilloes, Marsh. Peccadilloes. I've told you not to use words you don't know."

"Piccadilloes—peccadilloes—you've got them."

"It's publicity, Marsh, for the country club. I scarcely know the creature. We've got a financial campaign starting next week. It's business."

"I know the kind of business it is. You've got egg all over your face. And hers too. Where'd you pick her up?"

He was sitting near the "window" and they could see his eyes as they fixed on her a long moment, the flat, expressionless, calculating eyes of a poker player. "I have no intention, Marsh, of answering questions about this girl, except I will say she is a daughter of a very old friend of mine on The Row."

She got to her feet. "Don't give me that, Blitz."

"Come on, get dressed. We'll be late."

"Oh yes, 'come on.' I'm good enough to go with you to your crummy poker parties, but when it's——"

"Marsh! I told you——"

"You told *me*. I'll tell *you* something. I know what you're up to, and you're not going to get away with it."

She mashed out a cigarette. "I told you I wasn't clearing out. I've given you thirteen years and for what? Cheap apartments, cheap cars, cheap clothes, while you and your holier-than-thou mother——"

"If you ever again mention my mother——"

"I'll mention her any time I please."

He shrugged. "You leave me no choice——"

"Blitz—if you walk out on me——"

"If I do—what?"

The anger was such that it choked off her words. He went on, "I know what is going on in that little mind of yours. You intend to threaten me. You want to say you will inform on me. But you wouldn't do that, Marsh. No one would believe you. It would be your cheap word against mine."

He took her by a shoulder and pushed her toward the bedroom. "Now let's quit this, Marsh. Go on and get dressed."

Deliberately she lighted another cigarette. "I'm not going. Take that old con-woman mother of yours. So respectable—but twenty years ago you couldn't have taken her——"

She stopped suddenly, warned by what she saw in his eyes. As he swung an open palm she grabbed his wrist by one hand and broke the blow. Yet it still cracked hard against her face and rocked her.

She lashed out then in anger and hysteria, taking him by surprise, and in the shock of that surprise he fell back against the wall. She was on him, flailing at him. He caught her wrists and held them, but then in one sharp quick lunge, backed by all the strength in her body, she jerked free and jabbed the cigarette into his cheek. He screamed, and his outcry shocked her, and she stepped back, her eyes not believing what they saw.

Blinded with pain, his hands faltered for the nearest chair. He said, "Marsh, how could you?"

They met in Lancaster's office later that night—Greg, Joe Packer, and Bill Akers of Homicide.

Lancaster moved restlessly about the room, drawing short puffs on a cheap cigar.

"What do you think, Evans?" he asked.

The problem was whether to bring Ellen Marshall in for questioning. They would lay before her the evidence they had that she had acted as a courier, knowingly or unknowingly, and point out the long prison term a conviction would bring. They would suggest she turn "double agent." If she would return to the apartment and carry on in usual fashion and report Malone's plans to them and turn state's evidence when and if they arrested Malone, they would seek leniency for her.

"She hates him tonight," Greg answered, "but thirteen years of old ties and memories—well, she may be back in his arms tomorrow night."

"But if she knows she's going up," Packer put in, "she'll be thinking of herself first—and she might give us what we need to hang this on Malone."

Greg opened a window wider to clear the smoke. "I've got a suggestion. We take a certain risk if we bring her in, a good chance she'll double-cross us. I've got an angle on the highjacking deal. It may trap both Hoagy and Malone if it works. If it doesn't— well then . . ."

"Good," Lancaster said. "We'll wait. A few days won't matter."

Packer was let down. He would have enjoyed "breaking" Ellen Marshall.

CHAPTER 27

The night manager at the Meridian Hotel greeted Greg and Packer with a professional smile. He was a balding, thinnish man in his forties with a brisk, to-the-point manner. After identifying themselves they asked if he had a priest registered. He flicked hurriedly through the cards. "Yes. Father Bernard. Room 608. Would you like me to ring him?"

"No," Greg said—and then his heartbeat quickened. Walking straight toward them from the elevator bank was the Priest.

Greg said quickly, "Don't let on we've asked about him."

They walked away as the Priest placed his key carefully on the counter. They heard him say, "If anyone wants me, I'll be back in an hour." He had a low, soft way of speaking. He was an older man than Greg had anticipated, probably in his sixties with distinguishing gray hair. His face was the flabby, bland, lifeless sort that would fade into any crowd, perfect for his trade.

He passed them at the cigar counter while they were asking the redhead for cigarettes. They were conscious of the movement of his robe stirring the air. They stalled, chatting with the girl, who answered in bored monosyllables. They watched as he pushed his way through the revolving door and turned to the right.

As they started toward the street, Greg put a hand on Packer, slowing him. When they first had entered the hotel, Greg had noted a man sitting by a window, thoroughly engrossed in a newspaper. The man now came to life, getting to his feet with obvious intent of purpose. He tossed the newspaper back into the chair and walked swiftly toward the door. He, too, turned to the right.

Outside they spotted the Priest a half block away, moving briskly through a crowd of late showgoers and swing-shifters. The man was following him. He might be from a rival gang or he might be a "walking outpost," one of the Priest's own men trailing him to make certain no one was running a shadow job on him. Packer dropped back of Greg now for the same purpose.

They barely glanced in the direction of their own surveillance car. The lights came on in recognition. They knew the officer would wait until they were almost out of sight before pulling into the steady stream of traffic. Otherwise he would have to creep along and might be spotted by the "walking outpost."

The Priest paused to look in a window, the man behind him followed suit, and Greg did likewise. He assumed Packer was doing the same. It was like an old-fashioned farce; a surveillance job always was.

The Priest hurried on for another block. When he reached the corner, he joined a small group waiting for a bus.

The man turned back and retraced his steps. Greg continued his course, passing the man. The man's gaze fell briefly on him, but Greg knew he was looking everyone over.

Greg went beyond the bus stop. His problem now was to kill time. If he stopped before too many windows or reversed his steps, the man would become suspicious. He sauntered into an all-night drugstore, which was crowded, took a seat at the soda fountain so he could see out the door, and ordered ice cream.

Packer had joined the group at the bus stop and was standing alongside the Priest. That was a part of a well-run tail job. Let first one detective take the lead and then the other. Keep switching positions.

The Priest was a cool operator. He glanced about casually from time to time, taking stock, careful to avoid any pointed movement. He looked comfortably at ease in his cassock. The masquerade, of course, was not original with him. Several bank robbers had affected it during holdups and, on occasion, confidence men, the same as other criminals had disguised themselves as farmers, messenger boys, army generals, and delivery men. But these were in the minority. It had been some three or four years since Greg had worked a masquerade case. Except for the "con" men, the average criminal had little inclination to turn actor and little talent for it.

When the South Street bus slowed to a stop with a gush of air, the Priest held back. The driver was making change for his last customer, a heavy-set, talkative biddy, when the Priest stepped in. The doors closed smoothly behind him in almost the same instant, and the bus swung back into traffic.

Packer had glanced idly at the bus, but with several others continued standing, pretending he was waiting for another. He returned to reading a tabloid newspaper. And Greg continued with his ice cream.

Farther down the street the man climbed into a taxi, and a second later, a police car—a black nondescript sedan—moved up to the bus stop and barely hesitated. The driver had the door already open for Packer.

The surveillance car took off slowly in the wake of the taxi. Everything, everybody on a surveillance job, from the hunted to the hunter, were usually in slow motion, as though they were following old habit patterns.

Greg left the exact change with his check, strolled out to the curb, and a second police car picked him up.

"Don't let that streetcar block you," Greg said.

The officer had a drawl. "Not meaning any offense, but I was working tail jobs before you had your first Wheaties." He added, "I remember one I worked on a bicycle. A murder case. Cracked it, too."

The bus turned into South Street, a wide boulevard, and was set for a run of six miles. At the next corner the two surveillance cars left South Street, drove one block, and swung into Carol. They were now running parallel on Carol, with the bus on South.

Whenever the bus stopped, they watched from a block away. Each time the bus lights limned the Priest perfectly. He was sitting about midway and on their side. After the bus moved on, they would wait until the taxi trailing it passed.

As they had planned in advance, they were conducting a "loose" surveillance. It was so "loose" they might lose the Priest. But if they had decided on a "close" tail run, they might have tipped him off. On a "close" job, Packer would have boarded the bus and sat a few seats behind.

Greg felt the tautness in his stomach. He never yet had "lost" a man.

"Was he ever a priest?" the driver asked.

"Never."

"Glory be, I think he's taking an awful chance wearing the cloth. I'd hate to go up there and have to face the good Lord."

One block before the end of the bus run the Priest got off. From the parallel street they saw him in the aura cast by the feeble street light overhead. He appeared to hesitate and turned away from them, taking a side street. The taxi continued to trail the bus.

They now played a weaving game. One car would pass him as he trudged along, and proceed four to six blocks beyond him before turning, and then the other, approaching from the opposite direction, would work the same routine. They spaced their trips a few minutes apart. Whenever they lost him, they would weave the same way along streets he might have turned into, and each time they located him within two or three minutes.

After a short while it became evident he was following a pattern. His walk centered more and more about one certain block. He was studying the houses and the general lay of the land. It

122

was a suburban area with modest residences set far apart on acre tracts. The streets were quiet and lonely and darkened by ancient gnarled oaks, and there was a God's-in-His-heaven feeling. A light burned in an occasional picture window, offering a glimpse of a provincial or Early American setting. The area had a picturesque touch, too, rising steeply until each row of houses looked down on another row, in a terraced effect.

Eventually they located the "walking outpost," who had left his taxi. He, too, was weaving. He worked the opposite side of the street from the Priest, sometimes walking in the opposite direction and other times following him by a half block.

An hour of this stalking passed before the Priest returned to South Street. He waited twenty minutes for the bus, a lone figure beneath the street light. A block away, the man also waited.

The return to the hotel was routine, except for the exhilaration that had vanquished Greg's need for sleep. It would be easy tomorrow to learn who had moved recently into the neighborhood.

CHAPTER 28

The next day held its usual sweet-bitter mixture.

He left the house the same time Cyn did. She was running, a sign she was later than usual. She called, "Good morning," as though she herself had put the day together, and a deep longing rose as he watched her get into the car. She was a part of his life now, as though she always had been. Yet actually it was only since that night a couple of months back, when on impulse she had kissed him and fled.

Six little monsters—three boys and three girls. He wouldn't get to see much of them, not in his business, but they would keep him in form. He guessed he could take them, although Timmy multiplied by six was something to give a man pause.

He stopped off at Cokie Logan's apartment house to talk with the men on stake-out. The night hours had passed with deadly monotony—the kind where a man stays awake only through the agony of moving about or talking. And then it came out. They grumbled that Lancaster had pulled off the last radio car about 4:30 A.M. Inside Greg, the long slow pull he'd felt on the trigger these last days suddenly exploded.

She wasn't his girl—in that apartment—or his sister or anyone he cared for. She was only another of a thousand women his work would take him by that year, a name to be forgotten, a face that would fade until at last he wouldn't even be able to recall it. But it was as though she were Cyn, the way he felt that moment.

He slammed the car door and gunned the motor, hearing the tires screech as the car shot out. He was still trying to bring himself under control when he climbed the old worn steps at headquarters.

Lancaster was coming out of his office, a bantam rooster crossing the road. "Hello, Greg," he said, noting his anger. He continued hurriedly, "I had to pull a radio unit off the Logan girl this morning for a stake on the West Side. That knife prowler again."

He took a step around Greg. "Sorry I haven't time to talk. Politicians on my neck this morning. You understand."

His short legs took two steps to Greg's one, but he was fast, and he was gone before Greg could corner him. The man had an uncanny instinct for knowing men and what they were thinking and how to handle them.

Greg by-passed the elevator and took the steps down to Homicide. The walk cooled him. Lancaster had a job to do, a tough, grinding, battering, hopeless job. He was an army commander with too few men and too little equipment, rushing his forces here and there to try to hold the breach, knowing the most he could do was to contain the enemy, unable ever to mount an attack, always outnumbered.

And always the politicians on his neck, driving him, threatening him, holding out the stinking bait that one day he might be chief. If he lived that long.

Greg shook his thoughts off as he approached Homicide. At

the door he almost collided with Joe Packer. Packer asked permission again—for the tenth time—to question George Pierson, the private detective who had slugged Greg in Ellen Marshall's apartment that night.

Greg was adamant. "You can't trust him. He'd tip off Malone—wreck Malmo."

Packer thought not but Greg knew he was right. Pierson specialized in divorce cases. He brazenly offered to obtain "proof of unfaithfulness" for his clients. He had two girls working for him, "compromising" the husbands, and a gigolo for the wives.

From across the room Bill Akers called to Greg. "Where you been?" he asked. It was his favorite joke. If a man worked the clock around, he'd still want to know where he'd been. Greg laughed by rote.

Akers kicked a chair out for Greg to sit on and fished among the stacks of reports on his battered old desk for the funeral layout.

"Here's where we're spotting the men," he said, pointing to a diagram showing the church where in a few hours the last rites would be said for Jan Logan. The physical setup, which the police topographical section had prepared, showed every door and window of the church, as well as the houses in the immediate area, the alleys, the streets, even a storage mailbox where a man might conceivably hide.

"I don't see how a ghost can get to her," Bill Akers said, and Greg readily agreed, both knowing they were deceiving themselves, because a clever ghost could. Every plan had a flaw, if not in the actual mechanics, then in the timing.

Akers then handed him several teletypes from towns reporting on Mick Foster, Cokie Logan's boy friend. Either Foster had just left or hadn't been seen. They added up to a disturbing negative.

As they were finishing, a call came in from a deputy sheriff at Centralia, twenty-two miles east, advising that a man answering the description of Dr. C. Oxford Jones, the missing scientist, had registered at a motel the night before under the name of Robert C. Smith. His license number, as taken from a registration card he himself had filled out, was CL-75892. The make of car was a 1953 Ford hard-top, a gray-black combination.

As Greg left, the detectives began setting in motion the machinery that would enlist the co-operation of other police, deputy sheriffs, and the highway patrol.

He stopped in at Records to call the Tech. Old 66 hadn't breathed so much as a whisper, and he couldn't figure it.

He was going down the murky hall, conscious as always of the floor beneath him trembling, when he met McTamish. Mac probed in his easy way about the Logan case, as if it were a humdrum matter. Mac's theory was that if he could get a detective to talking the detective would drop something. And that, Greg admitted, was the premise he was proceeding on in the Malmo case. In the avalanche of words spilled by Old 66 he would find a key clue or a combination of thoughts and ideas.

"They tell me one of the dame's boy friends has disappeared," Mac said.

"Who told you that?" Greg countered.

Mac smiled. "People."

He had to have Mac if his plan was to work. He studied him now, realizing he didn't actually know the man though he had seen him around for years.

He might persuade Mac to his bidding if he promised him the inside on a big case or two, like the story that had jeopardized Cokie Logan's life. But that was out.

Surely there must be another way to appeal to him, something he wanted or took pride in. "You're getting pretty important," Greg said.

Mac was suspicious. "What do you mean?"

"The by-lines you're getting. I can't pick up a copy of the *News* without seeing your name."

"Oh, that. They pay me in by-lines. It's an old newspaper trick. You ask for a raise and they give you a by-line."

He was pleased nonetheless that Greg had noticed. "What you been doing since you left Homicide?"

"Working a detail for Lancaster."

"The scuttlebutt's that you're heading the Tech."

"The what?"

Mac shrugged. "I'd better be getting along. Be seeing you."

"Sure," said Greg. He was disturbed as he walked away. So Mac knew the department's most guarded secret, knew when he wrote that sentence, "The police acted on a tip," exactly where that tip had come from. Still, he hadn't given the secret away, and Greg puzzled why.

Mac was dangerous—and he desperately needed him.

CHAPTER 29

She sat curled up on the divan, waiting for Mick with a quickening, steady beat of her heart. She put aside Euripides and the horrible drama about Bacchus, knowing it was no use and if she were questioned in class tomorrow she would have to confess she hadn't read it.

Mick had said he would call for her at nine-thirty, and it was now close to ten. He seldom was late.

She heard the policewoman stirring in the bathroom, washing out lingerie. She was a part of her life now. She came at eight every night and slept in the other twin bed, which had been Jan's, with a revolver on the floor where she could reach it quickly. She said little but was pleasant.

Mick had phoned her at the restaurant around five-thirty. He had been in town several hours, he said, and had been trying to locate her. He couldn't talk long, some fellows were waiting. He was hesitant and stumbled when he mentioned Jan, and she loved him for his awkward sympathy. And all the time she could scarcely talk for the breathless happiness coursing through her.

Mick was all that she had now.

He had sounded hurried and disturbed, but she knew she had too, for how could you say what you had wanted to say all summer over a public telephone in three minutes?

Since the funeral she had returned to her old job at the restaurant and begun her junior year in college. She had awakened and eaten and walked and talked as if she were another person and she herself were standing off to one side, grieving and watching this other individual act as if nothing had happened, as if Jan were alive. Julia Bunker downstairs had said she was "brave," but Julia Bunker hadn't known.

And always there were the footsteps behind her, the detective who had become a part of her. He was there, waiting outside, when she left the restaurant at eight, just as the day was slipping into the night. He was there when she hurried out of the apartment a little after seven the next morning for the English lit class. She wasn't to look back at him, she wasn't to talk with him. She was to pretend he wasn't about. It was like being pushed back into childhood, a game to play with youngsters you didn't want at your house.

She started slightly when the phone rang. She almost caught her foot in the frayed corner of the dining-room rug on her way to pick up the receiver from the buffet. It was Gale. Every night about this time she called on the pretext of discussing class work. She no longer was real groovy with the sharp talk, nor frank with her opinions. She was hurt deeply—hurt because Cokie was. It was surprising, the friends whom she might have expected such warmth from who never gave it, and others like Gale who felt for you and, more importantly, with you.

The old wall clock in the dining room, which had been her mother's and her mother's before her, chimed ten-fifteen. She began to worry about Mick. He never would have been so late if something hadn't happened.

She glanced at herself in the old-fashioned oval mirror that also had been her mother's, found her compact, and began a repair job. She mustn't let Mick know her grief; she must give him the kind of a date they would have had if . . .

The policewoman startled her. "Excuse me, hon," she said. "I didn't mean to slip up on you."

"I guess I'm jumpy."

"I think I'll turn in. What about you?"

She asked it apologetically, as if to say, It's my job to ask.

"I've got a date. He should've been here by now."

"Will you be going out?"

"I don't know. We might."

The policewoman padded away toward the kitchen for a glass of milk. "Good night then, hon. Don't stay out too late."

She never intimated that Cokie was not free to go as she pleased. She merely inquired about her plans, and then when the door closed behind Cokie she would telephone and soon Cokie would become conscious of the man trailing her, his steps geared to her short ones.

The policewoman repeated her good night as she retraced her steps to the bedroom. Cokie stretched out on the divan, careful not to muss her white blouse, and closed her eyes. It was at night that the terror lay very real. During the day, in the hot glare kicked up by the pavements, it was a thought that lurked in the back of her mind, that the sunshine itself seemed to deny. But in the dark she would catch herself wondering guiltily about friends she had known for years.

The hard knock on the door was Mick's. She would have recognized it anywhere. In two steps she was in his arms, half swept up as he stepped in, kicking the door shut behind him, feeling his wind-burned lips on hers, his strong arms holding her until her lungs couldn't take it longer. All the aching, hurting yearning of the long summer found escape at last.

He was as good-looking, muscular, big-shouldered, and rawboned as she remembered, and Indian-brown. His hands had the roughness of the outdoors, and she didn't want them to let her go. But he was whispering, "Let's get out of here, Cokie," and she was saying, "Okay." She tried to smooth her hair back in place as he took her hand.

In the corridor he said, "Let's take the back way," and in that moment she would have done anything he wanted. He was half running with her, his hand still in hers, tugging her. They went down the back stairs so fast they might have tumbled, and into the alley, which was so dark it was like walking blind. A garbage can rolled away from them with a frightening clatter, and she heard a cat scampering out of their path.

"I'm out of breath, Mick," she complained, pulling him to a stop. "What's the idea?"

"The cops. I don't want them snooping after us. This is our night and I'm not going to share it."

She walked with him quietly down the alley toward a shaft of light at the far end, his strong fingers on her bare elbow guiding her. She began to have regrets. She shouldn't have avoided her "shadow." If something happened, if this was the night . . . But no, it was all right. She had Mick. He wouldn't have a gun, but he would know how to handle any situation.

"I hope I didn't worry you—being so late," he said. "They had me down at headquarters."

"Who? The police?" She was frightened.

"Yes, they wanted to know where I'd been—wanted names of people who had seen me."

"Gosh, Mick, I'm sorry. It's terrible—just awful."

At the street he stopped her. They stood silent, looking, listening. The corner light threw a weak glow, and across the street a driveway spotlight contributed. But otherwise the leafy tree branches meeting overhead closed in the darkness.

"Did you tell them I used to date Jan?" he asked.

"No—no, I wouldn't tell them that. You know I wouldn't."

"They knew it. They were hunting an angle. Maybe Jan had tried to stop you from seeing me, maybe she was jealous, and I had gotten mad and done it, and you found out. Golly, Cokie, I don't know what it's all about. It doesn't make sense. None of it."

He was walking her fast again, toward the ocean. "I tell you what," he said. "I borrowed a skiff from one of my frat brothers today. Let's get in it, get out where we can talk."

She caught a frantic note in his voice. She had the fleeting impression he was running—running from something or someone.

"I don't know, Mick," she said hesitantly.

He put an arm about her waist, pulling her close. "Golly, Cokie, I didn't think the summer ever was going to end. And you—I wanted to be with you so when I heard . . ."

They had reached the beach. Straight ahead, if they had taken to the sand, they would have come to the spot where Jan's body had washed up that night, where in her heart-pounding imagery she often saw the flashlights of the police, heard the cry of the sirens and the shouting and calling, and the silence as they lifted her body from the sand.

They took the old sunken boardwalk, meeting no one, hearing only their own steps, Mick's heavy and scraping a little, hers a mere tapping tattoo.

Mick didn't know. He wouldn't have brought her here if he had.

She held his arm tighter, half leaning on him, feeling the warmth of his body through his shirt, listening to his deep steady breathing.

"Did the cops ask you about me?"

"Yes, Mick—but they did about everyone I know."

"What did they want to know about me?"

"Oh, mostly where they could find you, where you'd been all summer."

He fell silent, and a moment later she said, "Let's try to forget it, Mick. For tonight."

"Let's," he agreed.

They turned right at the corner, and ahead of them the low, rickety pier stretched like a long bony finger with strings tied to it, the strings holding little bobbing boat shapes. The lulling murmur of the surf reached them. It had a soothing cadence all its own, slow and soft.

They said little, and what they had to say they whispered, as though this were not a deserted pier but crowded. She clung to Mick as her eyes fell downward, to the water battering the spindle sticks the pier was built on. Halfway out, the waves leaped for her, the spray wetting her ankles.

"How do you like her?" he asked, pointing to a neat white skiff with the name *Gypsy* painted in a bold blue across the bow. He bent down to pull the boat about.

She never knew how the man could have come so quietly and quickly upon them. They had thought themselves alone, and then suddenly he was there, a few feet behind them.

"I can't permit you to do that, Miss Logan," he said.

Mick rose, turning swiftly. She caught his arm to keep him from swinging on the detective.

CHAPTER 30

Greg's appointment with Dr. Meredith, the psychology professor, was for four. He was a few minutes late when he asked a student to direct him to the Liberal Arts Building.

He climbed steps that had been worn by the feet of several generations to a drab, gloomy second floor. Opening the door to Room 210, he paused a second in surprise. Dr. Meredith turned toward him from a file cabinet. She was a slender, well-designed blonde of about thirty with quick, bright eyes that openly appraised him.

"You weren't expecting a woman?" she asked.

"Dr. Jason didn't tell me——"

"He never does. It's his little joke. You can leave if you want to."

Greg put his reels of tape on her desk. She looked at them speculatively. "Frankly, I've never done anything like this."

"It may not work. Dr. Jason thought we might give it a try. I don't know what I'm hunting. But maybe there's something in all this dialogue—a behavior pattern. Maybe someone has given something away that I don't catch."

He outlined the background of Malmo, step by step. She said

she would have to work on the tapes nights, since she had no other time. She said she would call him when she had finished.

It was a little after six when he checked into the Tech. George Benson shook his head to indicate that Old 66 had garboed out again.

"Do you think somebody's tipped 'em off?" George asked. He handed Greg Old 66's log, which showed Hoagy had called Harry Malone at 7:27 A.M. and again at 4:23 P.M. Both conversations had been brief, and neither had mentioned Cokie Logan or the "they" who plotted to murder her.

"It just couldn't be," Greg answered. He said it confidently, as if to reassure himself. He was growing edgier each day under the ominous quiet that had come over 66.

And for another day, too, he had written "negative" on the report he had submitted to Lancaster on the O.W. setup into Marsh's apartment. Harry Malone had not been back, nor had he called her, nor had she phoned him since that night she had pushed the burning cigarette into his cheek. Malone had kept the incident to himself. He had explained the patch that covered his cheek by telling friends he had a skin infection "that might leave a scar." What he was thinking about Marsh was his own secret.

Greg walked around the horseshoe, glancing at the logs. He stopped before Tech 12. "Mrs. Andrews to Mrs. Peet—Personal—2:47 P.M."

"She may make it," George said, referring to Joan. "Poor kid, she wants one of those dolls you can wash their hair and they wet their pants."

Greg laughed and then stood a moment, held by a thought, before going to his desk. He saw at once the memo marked SPECIAL from Miss Cabot. Max Reed in Records wanted him to call. Reed's laconic hello was little more than a grunt. He was a sawed-off fellow who had been shunted in and out of a dozen offices before he had been hidden in Records.

"Oh yeah, I got something for you," he said. "I think it'll bowl you right off your pins. It's an ident on C. Oxford Jones. Thought you might be over this way."

Greg said he would. It was the first break on the missing scientist.

Before going to Records he kept a seven o'clock appointment with Lancaster to check the plan of operations for the next night, when the Priest and his mob would attempt to highjack the $400,-000 the Kansas City crowd had stolen from the Federal Reserve bank. It was a dangerous scheme Greg had laid out. It called for one man in the police raiding party to expose himself to "enemy" gunfire—without firing a shot in return. That man probably would be Greg. Lancaster offered no protest. He recognized that the "calculated risk" was worth taking for this one chance to crack Malmo.

Lancaster chewed on his cigar and studied Greg out of squinty, sharp eyes. "It just might work," he said, and added, "I'll take the responsibility."

He worked his cigar over a while. "About the grand jury tomorrow——"

"The call's for two o'clock," Greg said. "The D.A. tried for a postponement but couldn't get it."

Lancaster looked away. "Take a tip from an old police officer, Evans. Don't tell them any more than you have to. They can get out of hand."

Greg nodded but not necessarily in agreement, and Lancaster was quick to note it. "I've seen grand juries come and go. They can be dangerous. We haven't anything to hide—but there's no use stirring them up."

"I'll be careful," Greg promised. Lancaster was of the old school that believed a police officer should play it silent. Greg couldn't agree. If the department had nothing to conceal, why then hide the facts and arouse suspicions? The more open a police officer was, and the closer he was to the people, the more respect he would command.

Lancaster came around the desk to walk him to the door. "I'll handle things from this end myself tomorrow night," he said. "If we can get the breaks . . ."

The breaks so often decided it, and by the law of averages they fell as often to the criminal as to the department.

He had to wait a few minutes at Records. Max Reed was watching a run-through on an electronics machine that was sorting punched cards at the rate of six per second. The machine was looking for a suspected killer with the tattoo of a mermaid on his right arm. A clerk was feeding hundreds of cards into the robot, which was searching for the 19 punch, indicating a tattoo. The machine cracked better than nine hundred cases a year.

When Max, a brusque, busy little man, hurried over, Greg nodded to a new sign posted on the wall: WE SOLVE MORE CASES THAN ANY TWO SQUADS COMBINED.

"Wait till Lancaster sees that," Greg said.

"Lancaster be damned. If he'd give me another man we'd solve five more cases a week. Do you know what that would mean on the year-end statistics? If I could get more time myself . . ."

It was the same old plaint with every squad, every division. More time. Time was the great enemy.

Max Reed picked up the transcribed ident on Dr. C. Oxford Jones. "We haven't had a character like him around in years," he commented. "Absolutely unbelievable. Here's his record. Arrested New York, 1946, posing as Winston Churchill's personal emissary. Arrested Atlanta, 1947, posing as Lord High Mayor of London. Skipped bond that time. Warrant for arrest issued Boston, 1948, represented himself as English adviser to Haile Selassie, Emperor of Ethiopia.

"Oh yeah, here's where he became the world-famous scientist, Dr. C. Oxford Jones. Employed 1949 by University of Chicago, worked there three years, discharged quietly 1951. Employed 1952 by University of North Carolina, disappeared six months later."

He shoved the ident across the desk to Greg. "You know how we got it?" he asked. "One of the boys knew he'd seen that personnel file picture. He cut a master and ran ten thousand cards through, but nothing came out that looked good. So on his own time—his own time, mind you—he started going through the mug books. He found him in the seventy-eighth. If Lancaster would only give me another man . . ."

"Yes, I know," Greg said, studying the report. C. Oxford Jones, which wasn't his name at all, of course, belonged to that fabulous clan of masqueraders whose intelligence and often brilliance would have earned them an excellent living in everyday life if they had played it honestly. They were children in a way, children in a world of their own make-believe. His record was incredible. He had once delivered an impassioned plea before the United Nations as a representative of the Gold Coast. Another time he had represented himself as a White House adviser at an American bankers convention.

He never, though, had worked on the Manhattan Project. That was a part of his "scientific background," none of which was true, not even the country of his birth. Instead of being English, he was American, the son of a Greensburg, Pennsylvania, hotel owner.

Greg noted he never had been accused of a crime of violence. Max Reed spoke up. "He doesn't look like your man to me. Those guys don't usually kill. But you never can tell. I remember a case . . ."

He never got to finish. The phone call was for Greg. Julia Bunker was on the line, the "woman downstairs" in Cokie Logan's apartment house.

"Remember me?" she asked in a low, husky voice.

"Sure."

"I'm worried," she continued. "I glanced out the kitchen window a moment ago, before I turned the light on, and saw a man standing in the little patio. You know, the one near the fire escape that passes Cokie's bedroom window."

"Yes, I remember."

"It was dark, but he walked into the light once, and I think he's the same man I saw earlier tonight coming down from upstairs."

Greg asked a few questions, thanked her, and was about to hang up when she said, "Will you drop by, Mr. Evans? I have something else I think you should know."

He sat a second in thought. "Something?" Max Reed asked.

"Might be." He telephoned Cokie's apartment, heard her answer, and without identifying himself asked to speak with the policewoman. Afterward he notified Homicide and called Joe Packer, who was comfortably settled by the television, watching wrestling.

They met at the apartment house. Homicide already had posted two detectives in a radio car a block away on a dark side street. He and Packer, hugging the shadows, reached the car, and the four plotted the setup for an all-night stake-out. He left then to talk with Julia Bunker.

She opened the door cautiously and then offered a warm, firm hand.

"I'm so glad you came by," she said. She was in a wispy sheer negligee that was a pink billow. Her hand went to the plunging V to pull the lacy border together. She had let her soft wavy brown hair down, and it was cascading about her shoulders, giving her a bedtime look.

"Sit here, won't you?" She indicated the divan. She sat at the other end, turning toward him and doubling her knees half under.

She told him about a call Panther Wilson had made on Cokie. He only half listened. He already had had a report from the policewoman.

As she talked, she slipped a little farther down in the cushions in a yawny, relaxed pose. Her arms went gracefully behind her head, drawing the negligee sheer and tight about her.

The invitation was there—in her eyes, her voice, on her full lips. Warm and eager and dreamy. A woman need never say it. It was in the faint flower scent, the soothing murmur of her talk.

"How about a drink?" she asked.

"No, thanks," he said, feeling the deep tiredness of the hammering, hectic, frustrating day fall away.

She moved across the room to a television bar and poured for herself, glass clinking on glass.

"What about the man in the patio?" he asked.

She held her eyes on his as she put the decanter back, and then a little-girl-in-mischief smile stole into them. It confessed there had been no man in the patio.

"What about the man here?" she asked in a husky whisper. Her body was taut and very straight. She returned to the divan and stood near him, looking down with a faint smile about her lips, waiting.

He rose slowly and walked past her to the door. She was sipping her drink, watching him, her face now a shell.

"I'm sorry," she said.

"I'm flattered you went to all the trouble," he answered.

"You've got a girl?" she asked.

"In a way."

"You're engaged?"

He smiled back at her. "I'd like to be."

The sheer exhaustion of one day added to another was upon him as he returned to the radio car. He cut diagonally across at the corner, passing directly under the street light. They were watching him as he came up, curious.

"Might as well call it a night," he said. "Nothing to it."

He didn't explain further, and what was all right with the head of Malmo was okay by them. He walked with Joe Packer to his car.

"Good night, Joe—I'll see you in the morning. Nine o'clock."

He continued down the street a couple of blocks to his Studebaker. As he was getting behind the wheel he discovered he was out of cigarettes and recalled having passed a drugstore. He retraced his steps, almost in slow motion.

He remembered later that as he entered the store he was dully conscious there was someone in the phone booth, but at the moment he had only the cigarettes in mind. The druggist called from behind the pharmacy cubicle that he would be right out, and Greg idly looked over the cosmetics, thinking Cyn might like a box of bath powder. He heard a muted faraway name spoken, "Mac," and turned toward the phone booth. A showcase on top of a counter blocked his vision. Now that he concentrated he picked up what the man was saying, "Just another stake-out, Mac, that's about all."

The druggist came up behind him. "Sorry you had to wait," he apologized, but Greg was walking away from him.

Joe Packer was sitting in the booth, his hat on the back of his head and his lips close to the mouthpiece. Again he said, "Mac," and it was like a whiplash. Greg gave the door a vicious tug and it hammered its moorings with a crash. As Packer swung about, shocked, Greg's hands were on him. He dragged him from the booth and heard the receiver hit the wall a hard crack. The receiver continued to crackle with Mac's voice and the druggist shouted.

Greg held Packer before him for one brief second, with Packer yelling at him. And then Packer, like an enraged animal cornered, brought his right up savagely. Greg ducked and swung a driving blow to his chin. Packer went crashing backward into the cosmetics case and lay there stunned, a jagged gash in his head from which blood was spurting.

Greg walked out. He was shaking for the first time in years. A man couldn't work a hundred cases with another man, sit all night freezing in a car on surveillance, raid a flophouse where a killer might come out blasting—and not feel the shock of having lost a comrade.

It was like Joe Packer had died.

CHAPTER 31

The D.A. stepped aside to hold the door open. As Greg entered, the jurors sized him up, neither hostile nor cordial. They numbered twenty-three and were hand picked, each having been appointed by a Superior Court judge. Among them were a druggist, a doctor, a factory foreman, a Parent-Teacher's president, a department-store saleswoman, an electrician, a retired professor, and a builder.

"Sit over here, Greg, please," the D.A. said, and Greg took a raised witness chair. The jurors themselves were stair-stepped to his left.

The D.A. walked before them and they fell quiet. "The police chief has named Lieutenant Evans to answer your questions," he said. Their eyes brushed the D.A. aside and stayed with Greg and were inert, expressionless. For forty-seven days they had been in session. By now they knew all about the other fellow, where he worked, how many children he had, whether he mowed his own yard, what he thought of the world situation. They had become a neighborhood in a sense, and the usual pattern of close bonds as well as suspicions and enmities had developed.

"I must remind you," the D.A. continued, "that Lieutenant Evans has a major case about to break, and if you will keep your questions short . . ."

The way they stirred indicated they hadn't bothered to listen. This was their show. The D.A. had had his. They had returned eighty-two indictments to date for him after hearing witnesses called by him and his deputies. Their job was to return an indictment—and hence begin the process of bringing a party to trial—if there was "reasonable evidence" to indicate a crime had been committed. And while their task primarily was to consider cases presented by the D.A., they had the right, too, to initiate their own and summon their own witnesses. The D.A. had attempted to channel their activities, but they had proved rambunctious. Already they had poked alarmingly into gambling and prostitution situations.

The foreman brought his long, thin frame up. He was well in his years, with a sparrowy, sharp-eyed look. "If the district attorney has no objections," he said softly, "we'd like him to step out."

The D.A. turned toward Greg with a glance that was a shrug. Greg crossed his legs, careful to avoid ruining the fresh crease in his trousers, and turned toward them.

"Dr. Buntin will begin the questioning."

Dr. Buntin cleared his throat and Greg singled him out. He was a short, waddling man with a cherubic face to match, a political-science professor at the university and a recognized authority on government.

He took an easy manner. "Lieutenant Evans, what is your position with the police department?"

"I'm working a special detail out of Assistant Chief Lancaster's office."

"Specifically, what does your detail do?"

"We're in charge of developing information through technological means."

Dr. Buntin peered over his glasses. He asked sharply, "You mean wiretapping?"

The others leaned a little forward. He could read their faces: Would he deny it, or would he hedge?

"Yes, sir—in part."

"You admit then that the police department engages in wiretapping?"

"I take exception to the word 'admit,' Dr. Buntin."

The foreman spoke up. "I think we can skip words like that."

"Very well. I would read you a pertinent sentence from the Fourth Amendment—the Bill of Rights: 'The right of the people to be secure in their persons, houses, papers, and effects, against unreasonable searches and seizures, shall not be violated.' Don't you consider, Lieutenant, that the police department should respect the Bill of Rights?"

It was a loaded question. "I understand there is a sharp difference of opinion over whether technical surveillances—as we call them—violate the Bill of Rights."

"Don't you consider that a wiretap violates 'the right of the people to be secure in their persons' and is in a way a 'search' by a listening device?"

"I'm a police officer, Dr. Buntin. I leave that to the courts."

A brawny man of about thirty, with a face hewn sharply down the sides, spoke up from the first row. "Let's get on with it, Dr.

Buntin. We're not here to debate a hypothetical question. We know everybody wiretaps."

He looked at Greg. "Isn't that right, Lieutenant? By the way, I'm Sam Adams—Adams Pharmacy."

"Yes—every law-enforcement agency in a community of any size does, and that includes the police, the sheriff's office, the state investigators. And of course the federal ones in Washington——"

"Even if it's against the law?" Dr. Buntin asked.

"Yes, sir. But it's not against the law in this state. I might add that it is illegal in some states."

Adams cut in, "Do you wiretap on everything?"

"No—only in cases of extreme violence."

Dr. Buntin asked, "But you could put a wiretap on a private citizen who hadn't done anything?"

"I've never known that."

"Not even a politician the police department wanted to spy on?"

"No, sir."

"But you surely realize the evil that could be done by an unscrupulous police chief or officer?"

"Yes——"

"Did you know that it was done in Paris in 1939 and many people consider that it hastened the fall of the government at the time of Hitler's invasion?"

"What are we getting at?" Adams interposed. "The question here is, are the police abusing wiretapping?"

The foreman spoke up. "Yes, let's get down to actual cases, Dr. Buntin."

Dr. Buntin whitened. "Please, I beg your indulgence. This is a question of a man's basic freedom—whether he can sit down in his own home and feel it is his home and nobody can come into it. I would quote you from George Orwell's novel, *1984*—that one of these days we'll live on the assumption that every sound we make is being overheard."

Adams said, "Oh, nuts. I don't give a hang who listens in on my telephone if it's going to keep a kid from being kidnaped—or someone from getting killed."

"Look," the foreman said, "I'd suggest——"

Dr. Buntin interrupted. "One more question. What about the other party on the telephone—the innocent party the criminal calls?"

"Yes, we hear his side of the conversation."

"If you introduce the recording into court—what he said to the criminal—and perhaps he doesn't have any idea he was talking to a criminal—well, isn't that an encroachment on his privacy—to have his words given the public when he didn't even know——?"

"Dr. Buntin—again, I'm not here to pass on the moral principle involved."

"But——"

"Please, let me finish." He wiped the sweat from his face. "I want to say that a conscientious officer tries to do what the law says and the people want. But here in this business of wiretapping we have Congress, the legislatures, the courts, the newspapers, and the people—all unable to decide what's right. And the confusion's even worse than that. A court makes a decision one year and reverses itself the next."

"What's your thinking about it?" Adams asked.

The foreman raised his voice. "I tell you——" Several jurors broke in. "Let him answer. We want to know."

Dr. Buntin said, "You know what he's going to say."

Greg started off haltingly, thinking Lancaster surely would have his neck if he found out. "Well, as I said, most people don't know what to think, but we do have two groups with definite ideas. We've got one that believes wiretapping has the seed in it for destroying all democratic government, while most law-enforcement officers want unrestricted use of it."

He hesitated and then continued, not sure of himself but wanting to say it because it was something that for a long time had pressed to be said. "I think wiretapping—uncontrolled—could become pretty frightening. And that's what we have now. You can go to any private detective—anywhere in the United States—and for three hundred dollars a week you can get a tape recorder put on anybody you name or a television camera secreted in an office or a bedroom, televising everything you do on a screen somewhere. Corporations are hiring detectives to spy on competing outfits, and politicians on other politicians, and lawyers on opposition lawyers. I don't believe most people have any idea how widespread it has become. And under our present laws nothing much can be done about private wiretapping."

He paused, and the quiet in the room jarred him. They didn't know yet where he stood. "As for wiretapping by the police, I've watched day after day as one horrible crime after another has been solved—and sometimes the criminals have been stopped before they could perpetrate the crime.

"People ask me, 'Why don't the police catch them as they always have done—by shadowing them?' Well, I'll give you an example. We have a case now where the two criminals never meet, and haven't for years. They do all their planning over the phone. So a shadow job wouldn't get us anywhere. And this isn't an isolated case—not among the big-time operators. My point is this: I don't think in this age of technological progress you can deny the police access to something the killers have."

"I've heard that a hundred times," Dr. Buntin interjected. "The police see only their own problem—not the broader one of personal liberty."

Adams said curtly, "Let him finish."

Greg nodded toward Dr. Buntin. "I agree with Dr. Buntin that the police are inclined to lose sight of the broader issue."

A stirring of feet and bodies answered him. "But that is only human nature," Greg said.

Lancaster wouldn't like this, not at all.

He spoke slowly and carefully. "I think certain definite controls should be placed over wiretapping by the police, so that it couldn't be used for evil purposes by unscrupulous officers. Maybe we could use the same procedure we do when we want to search someone's home. We have to get a warrant from a court, and the courts have been careful to guard the freedom of personal privacy in issuing search warrants. Maybe we could do the same in wire-tapping. Before we could use it, we would have to get court per-mission and offer reasonable evidence that a crime either had been committed or was in the process of being committed."

He added, "And of course all private wiretapping should be out-lawed—with heavy fines and long prison sentences."

No one said a word. Lancaster, of course, when he heard, would grumble, "What else could you expect from a cop out of a univer-sity?"

Dr. Buntin inquired, "What about installing microphones? Isn't that 'breaking and entering'?"

Greg winced inwardly as the old sore spot was rubbed. "I think the same—court permission——"

As he said it, he wondered whether he was right, whether a "bug job" didn't involve a more basic problem of personal liberty than a wiretap on a telephone.

Dr. Buntin settled back, and the foreman regained control of the panel. He began the interrogation, getting down to specifics. He wanted to know the nature of each case in which wiretapping was employed. Without using names, Greg supplied the informa-tion. Others came in, too, with their questions. Most of their in-quiries revolved about closed cases and whether innocent parties had been harmed.

Two hours later the foreman thanked him and excused him, and he left, feeling more drained than if he had been working a tough case. In his own mind he could see no evidence that there had been any abuse by the police of wiretapping. But with a grand jury—well, as the D.A. said, no one ever knew.

CHAPTER 32

That night a hot, suffocating stillness hung heavy over the city, so withering that it was a city crushed of all vitality. Everyone remarked it was earthquake weather, but no one believed it.

"It was this kind of a night when we took Bull Masterson back in '41," Bill Akers said. "I remember when we left this room—this same room—we felt something wasn't right about it."

Masterson had slain four officers, surprising them with a tommygun burst from the rear as they lay in ambush. Their names were on the plaque that hung in the far south end of the second-story hall, a plaque undusted since nailed up.

Bill Akers' reminiscing ended when Lancaster walked in at 7 P.M. sharp and took up a position behind his desk. He saw before him the department's eighteen ace detectives, veteran men who had stood up coolly to shotgun blasts and rifle fire on many another night such as this. Lancaster had pulled them in from many details. He took gruff, unspoken pride—and so did they—when people referred to them as Lancaster's Raiders.

He took an experimental puff on a new cigar as he turned to a photograph blown up to wall size. "This is the layout here," he said. "The Kansas City mob's been holed up in this house. We don't know what they're waiting for or what their plans are—and it doesn't matter. But we do know the highjackers will move in at 11 P.M. We'll let them—and if a gun battle breaks out between them we'll wait till it's over. I want every man to understand that, because Operation Malmo depends on it. Nobody will move until the signal's given. And I want you to understand this——"

He waited until every man was looking his way. "—if one of the highjackers gets the money and makes a break for it, we're going to let him escape. Is that clear?"

It was a strange situation, and while they made no sense of it, none asked any questions. If that was what the Old Man wanted, that was it.

"All right, Evans, let's have the details."

Greg stepped over feet and threaded past chairs to make his way to Lancaster's desk. Again he had the same uneasy feeling as in the grand jury room, because they were all watching him, the older men thinking he was too young for the Malmo assignment.

He began by mentioning a danger they would encounter tonight that they never had before. "The highjackers have been running constant surveillances, which means they'll probably have men spotted around tonight. It will be like a battle in which the enemy has filtered through your lines. We'll not only have the 'enemy' in front of us but also around us and perhaps at our rear."

He pointed to a blow-up with a pencil. "We've worked it out so that every man will be under cover. You will be posted either in a garage or in a neighbor's house. We've also had to station the radio cars considerably farther away—so that if the highjackers are using a 'floating car' to case the neighborhood the radio cars will be out of its cruising range."

He talked until he saw it was almost eight o'clock, noting detail after detail, answering questions, and changing the plan occasionally as somebody offered a better idea. Before he quit he ran over the criminal records of the Kansas City mob and the highjackers— which was a part of the psychological preparation. Raids became so commonplace, after working a few, that men were inclined to grow careless, to think themselves indestructible and take chances. It was well to remind them that those they hunted had slain others. It was well for each man to carry fear.

As the meeting was breaking up, a detective in the back spoke up. "I want to get one point straight. We're to let the highjacker with the money escape. All right. But what if he comes straight at one of us, blazing?"

Lancaster regarded him soberly. "I know it's a lot to ask," he said slowly, "but don't under any circumstances return fire."

A few hours before, Greg had located McTamish at Ace's Bar, having his first drink. Greg had asked him to step into Ace's office, a cluttered broom closet well plastered with pictures of chorines and models.

Mac brought his glass with him and fell into an old-time wicker chair while Greg pushed aside papers to sit on the desk.

"What d'ya want, Evans?" he asked, unhappy at being uprooted from his favorite bar stool.

Greg began cautiously, filling Mac in on the background of Malmo without naming names. Mac studied him cagily, waiting for the pay-off. When Greg reached it, Mac finished his drink slowly and shoved himself up.

"I don't go for it," he said.

Greg moved between him and the door. "You're going to hear me through, Mac."

"Don't try to throw your weight around, Evans."

"I'm not throwing any weight. I'm asking you to let me finish."

Mac sat down with a shrug. "I'm not faking any story, Evans—for you or anyone else."

"Except yourself?"

"What do you mean by that?"

"What about the Carson case?"

"Okay, so I dramatized it a little."

"That's all I'm asking you to do. Nothing more. And the next day you can fill in the details."

Greg took a tight hold on himself. This was it, the throw of the dice, the spin of the wheel. "We'll give you credit for solving one of the biggest crime stories in the country. It's the kind of a deal *Time* magazine writes up in its press section. You'll be in *Editor and Publisher,* maybe up for a Pulitzer nomination. You'll be a national figure—like Winchell was when that gangster surrendered to him personally rather than the FBI."

Mac was listening. "What about Joe Packer?" he asked.

"He's put in for a transfer to the Harbor Division."

"Are you going to prefer charges?"

Greg felt the exhilaration race through him. Mac was making

a deal. "No, Mac," he said. "I handle my own problems in my own way."

A sly smile took shape with Mac. "You're offering me a by-line, aren't you? I guess that's why you're a hell of a detective. You don't miss much."

"You don't yourself. What about it?"

Mac got up and stretched. He had a pleased look in his eyes.

As Greg walked away, he thought of all the other newspaper people he knew. They would have gone along solely on the basis of the justice at stake. But not Mac. He saw the one-column picture in *Time*.

Greg phoned Cyn, asking her to take in the mail and the milk, and heard the quiver of concern in her voice. . . .

The faraway cry of a baby seemed suspended in the stillness, and the feist-like yap of an unhappy dog. Closer by, muted drama poured from a television set, and then Greg heard tires yelp a little as a car took a corner too rapidly. The car's lights caught him up, seemed to waver, and then were gone. It wasn't one of the department's cars; it was someone else checking.

The leaves crunched softly under his feet, and he heard a second crunching, matching perfectly his steps but overlapping them. His feet picked up tempo. Those behind him skipped a beat and then matched his again. His right arm fell straight, swinging slightly, feeling the holster.

He walked on, never looking back, until the footfall behind him turned off. Climbing the hill then, he approached the house—tonight's "target"—from a higher elevation, slowed his walk, and listened intently. Certain he was alone, he struck off down an alley, keeping close to a hedge taller than his head. He stopped once as he heard the groan of a back door's hinges. There followed the clink of a milk bottle on concrete and the door closing.

When he was even with the house's front entrance, he stepped into the hedge. Bending low, he found the phone Termie Sanders, the bug man, had left him. He dropped flat and slithered across the ground, hot and parched from the day's sun, unwinding the

149

phone wire as he went. Once he heard the sickening squash of a snail as he dragged over it.

Laboriously he worked his way to a clump of shrubs under a front window. His view commanded the front entrance and the street beyond. The shades were drawn, but through the screened open window he could hear sounds from the living area. Before he could get settled, a low warning growl sounded directly over his head. The growl took him by surprise, since the surveillance report had read: "No dogs on premises."

A man's steps sounded then, crossing the room, the steps growing more definitive as he approached the window. "What's eatin' you, Duke?" Greg lay still, the old war training flooding back into his mind, and remembered to breathe deeply and slowly. His heart lurched when he wondered if the man could see him if he looked down.

With the man beside him, the dog muttered rather than growled. "Anything wrong, Al?" a woman called from another room, and the man answered, "Cat, I guess."

"Come on," he said. "You're not going catting tonight." He walked back into the other room, and the dog's low talking went with him. "This fool houn's no good," the man said, and the woman cried, "For criminy's sake, I'm trying to watch this movie."

Greg whispered into the phone, "Man and woman in dining room watching television. Dog also in house. I haven't been able to locate other two men."

He raised his head a few inches to take a quick reckoning. Through the shrub he could see across the street to a delivery truck parked in a neighbor's driveway. On its side was painted: "French Cleaners." That was the operations center, housing the monitor who would call the signals. Greg's phone connected with him. At the street corner, high up on the telephone poles, were the loud-speakers and the spotlights, which Termie had installed two days before in full daylight. He had dressed as a lineman and camouflaged them. Few people looked at a light pole, and none ever questioned what was up there.

High on the hill back of the house, he knew, was a small moving van. They had parked it in a driveway each night for a week, so that it would become a customary part of the scenery. When the time came, a small window in the back of the truck would open and the telescopic lens of a police television camera would poke its snout out. Another television camera peered down from the second story of the house across the street. Between the two they covered every foot of the area.

He heard two men crossing the living room. "I don't like it a damn," said one.

Their voices trailed off. Above the muted jabber of the television he heard talking and the clink of glasses as someone passed drinks around, and occasionally a man's laugh that came unrestrained from the belly. He counted the voices—four—and reported into the phone.

The night lay quietly then, stirred only occasionally by a car passing. It was considerably after eleven when the faintest whisper of an alien sound disturbed the pattern. The sound emerged eventually as footsteps. He took a deep breath to break the trigger tension, and then through a break near the roots of the shrubbery he saw the Priest coming up the winding sidewalk. His walk was relaxed and slow.

Inside, the dog growled. Once more Greg heard the man walking across the room and the scratching of the dog's toenails.

The Priest paused momentarily on the small entry porch and looked casually about. There was a corresponding silence inside, as though man and dog were listening. And in the quiet Greg became conscious of soft, approaching footsteps in the yard behind him. He assumed they belonged to one of the Priest's men; he dared not risk a movement to look over his shoulder.

The Priest pressed the bell, and when the soft chimes sounded, the dog gave a low bark. The door scraped the weather stripping slightly. "I wonder if I might use your phone?" the Priest asked. "My car's broken down."

The woman called from the dining room, "Who is it, Al?"

The man at the door said, "Sure, Father, come on in."

As the door closed, Greg heard the sharp cutting of screen wire behind him. Turning his head, he saw the man lift the screen out and climb in.

"The phone's here, Father," the man inside the house said.

The Priest's voice was soft. "I won't be needing it now."

"What the——" A gun butt cracked against a skull and a body crumpled to the floor. Almost quietly, it seemed to Greg.

The woman screamed, and two shots snapped with no more explosion than a whip cracking. A man's song suddenly rose in crescendo, booming through the house, as the television was turned up.

Greg said into the phone, "Woman screamed, two shots fired."

The pounding of horses' hoofs sounded now, but alien noises told Greg they were searching the house. He heard the rattle of things spilled from drawers, the hammering of furniture, the ripping up of the floor, and eventually the Priest's voice, sharp, forceful, commanding, "Here it is."

The sound went suddenly dead. A moment later the front door scraped. The Priest came first. He set a large suitcase on the concrete and straightened his cassock. Another man joined him. They looked about, unhurried, confident. Inside, the light went off and two more men materialized unexpectedly. Not a word was spoken.

Greg took a chance. He whispered into the phone, "Stand by . . ."

One of the men said, "I heard something." He snapped on a flashlight and beamed it in the shrubbery.

The Priest grabbed it. "Get hold of your nerves," he said. . . .

In the police truck, the monitor tensed as Greg's whispered words came over.

He repeated into the telephone hookup that linked the waiting detectives, "Stand by."

He sat in a miniature television control booth. Before him were two television receiving sets that would bring in the images broadcast from the moving van on the hill and the second story of the house across the way. It was a police setup strictly, on a police channel. Twice before they had used the technique with considerable success. By scanning the two receiving sets, the monitor could see the entire "playing field." He could keep the detectives posted over the loud-speaker on the whereabouts of each criminal. If a criminal sought to slip up on an officer, using the corner of a house as a shield, he could warn him. If an officer was walking into the range of fire, he could stop him. The television cameras could see where the raiders on the ground could not.

Greg's whisper, blown up on the volume, bounced about the walls. "Zero. Repeat, zero."

The monitor leaned toward a mike. "Zero—repeat, zero."

In a dramatic burst of light the giant spots from their anchors high on the poles flooded the area. On the television screens the monitor saw the Priest and his men caught in the intense light halfway down the sidewalk. They hesitated, stunned for a second by the startling development.

The monitor said over the loud-speakers, "We're police officers. We have you surrounded."

The four broke into flight, pairing off. The Priest struck off across the lawn for the shelter of the hedge and the alley. Greg, standing now, moved swiftly along the house, paralleling the Priest and his companion step by step.

The loud-speaker boomed out, "Two men heading for A. Two men for C." A was the southwest corner of the lot; C was the alley, covered by officers in a garage higher up the hill.

"C—watch your fire. Evans moving into your range. Plan 10 now in operation at C."

Plan 10 was the code signal to let the Priest out of the closing trap—and Greg with him, trailing him.

At the hedge the Priest fled down the alley toward the street. The other gunman headed up the alley toward Greg, who was coming down on the other side of the hedge.

"Evans! Evans!" was all the monitor had time to call. Greg dropped flat to the ground and waited while the gunman passed within three feet. Greg would let the officers in the garage higher up the alley take him.

The monitor said, "C—stand by—stand by—20 feet . . . Calling B. Move in toward A. All clear, Evans."

Greg rose swiftly and continued his course, running, bent over almost double. The Priest, at the street, changed his mind at the sight of a radio car and reversed his flight. He turned so suddenly that Greg was on him before the monitor could call out. The Priest fired as Greg again flattened himself. The Priest was running past him, firing as he went. The slugs ripped the ground about him.

"C—C—hold your fire—hold your fire. Take cover—take cover."

The monitor saw Greg on his feet again, stealthily trailing the Priest, trailing him past the garage that covered C, climbing higher and higher with him. . . .

The Priest turned right at the top of the hill. Below, Greg heard the crack-crack of gunfire for a moment longer, and then as he stayed behind the Priest by better than a half block all was quiet. Up here a few porch lights had come on, and neighbors were asking each other if they had heard gunfire, and doubting it.

The Priest walked at a fast clip for three blocks and turned down the hill. He looked back occasionally, but Greg kept switching from one side of the street to the other and hugging the shadows close to the houses. Near South Street the Priest vanished in a blotch of dark. A second later, as Greg was beginning to fear he had lost him, a car's lights blinked on as it swung away from the curb. Almost the same instant a blacked-out radio car that had been trailing Greg came alongside and he slid into the front seat.

"Keep your lights off until we get to South Street," he told the officer, a rugged young fellow whose face showed he was set for excitement. "And hold about a block behind him until we get into traffic."

The car ahead ignored the stop sign, taking the corner without slowing, and turning toward the city.

"Looks okay," the officer remarked.

"Can't tell. When he catches his breath he may get to wondering how he managed to escape—and if he changes his plans . . ."

"His ego won't let him," the officer said. "He'll think it was all because he was so blasted clever. Look at him go."

The mileage climbed to fifty and then sixty. The clear sweep of the street offered an unbroken speedway. If he looked back, and he surely would, wouldn't he suspect? But there was no other way.

The wail of a siren jabbed sudden fear into them. Ahead, a police traffic car shot out from a side street to give chase. The Priest's car had run a red stoplight.

"What's your number?" Greg asked, picking up the radio phone. It was this, the unexpected, the bad break, that you couldn't plan for.

"Six seven eight."

The Priest's car picked up speed with a jackrabbit jump, weaving dangerously around an occasional vehicle.

Radio Operations came on. "Come in, 678."

"Evans reporting—on Malmo. Traffic car on South Street, license plates E-67542, giving chase to our key subject. Will you call off? Ask officer to make it look like he was being outdistanced."

Now more cars loomed up suddenly before them as they neared the city, but the pace never slackened. The siren continued to fill the night with its fright. The traffic car was gaining on the Priest. The officers would be taking shots any minute at the tires.

And then with a sag of relief Greg heard the siren's wild plaint gradually trail off. The traffic car pulled over, and as they passed, the driver waved a hand. Two blocks later the Priest's car took a reckless right turn, almost climbing the sidewalk.

"It looks okay," the officer said.

It was okay. The Priest had turned in the direction of Hoagy's apartment house. Perhaps the siren and the chase had been all to the good. The Priest hadn't had time for thought.

They deliberately dropped farther behind and, two blocks from Hoagy's, quit for a side street. The setup in the area was much the same as at the scene of the raid. Detectives watched from neighboring apartments. Radio cars cruised in a radius of a few blocks.

Leaving the officer to park, Greg hurried to an apartment building five doors from Hoagy's. He took a hasty reckoning of the street, which was lined with imposing, many-storied structures in French château, timbered English, and Italian Renaissance styling. They jutted upward a few feet back from the sidewalk, forming a canyon.

At the far end of the first corridor he tapped, slipping a key at the same time into the lock. Termie Sanders was sitting Japanese-fashion on the bare floor of a linen closet before a playback machine.

"Hello, Greg," he said.

"How is it?"

"So-so. Room's got too much bounce. Any trouble?"

"Not much."

A field phone Termie had strung up buzzed. It was Operations Center calling from an apartment directly across the street from Hoagy's. "The Priest just drove into the garage."

The garage was a basement one, spread-eagled under the building. The Priest either would take the elevator or the stairs at the back to Hoagy's apartment, which was on the first floor, at the front of the building. It was a strategic location that gave Hoagy ready access to the street or, by going out a window, to the narrow labyrinth between the apartments.

"Where'd you put the mike?" Greg asked.

"Under the carpet. It's wall-to-wall."

"What if he steps on it?"

"He can't hurt it and it's too thin for him to notice."

The playback had the hum of a beehive. Termie hit it with his fist and it quieted. Then it came alive.

"Lock the door behind you." That was Hoagy's voice. "Hey, you look the same as when I last saw you."

He had no fear, no apprehension even. "I was getting worried about you."

"Had to kill the dog and the woman. Tied up the other two."

Hoagy's chuckle jarred the playback. "I bet it just broke you up,

156

shooting the dog. I remember—put it over here. We'll count it right here."

"The police were laying for us as we came out."

"How'd they know?"

"Guess someone heard the shots—but we had the TV up."

"Nobody followed you?"

"No, not here. I set a trap before I came in."

"Okay, let's get with it. By thunder, Zump, you're good for sore eyes."

The playback was quiet a few minutes. Greg squatted beside Termie, his legs drawn awkwardly under him, the air close with their breathing.

His eyes were held by the playback. It was a part of a bug setup, a vital part. Could anyone consider it a monster tonight? Could any court rule they were guilty of "breaking and entering," that in the meaning of the Bill of Rights they had jeopardized the "right of the people to be secure in their person"? Hoagy's right had been, of course, but did a human being preying on others by strangulation and knifings and shotgun blasts have a claim to such immunity?

He started when Hoagy spoke up. "Okay, it checks. What about yours?"

"I'm short a couple thousand."

"Count it again. You never were any good at figures. While you're doing it, I'm going to examine a bill or two. Not that we don't trust you—but the boss, he said to. You understand? He's always scared of getting counterfeit. He wouldn't touch counterfeit at any price."

"Go ahead."

Another short silence ensued. Termie tried to slap a moan out of the playback. "This thing's going to conk out someday in the middle of a murder," he said. "Department won't give me a nickel for new stuff."

Hoagy repeated how glad he was to see the Priest as their voices moved away from the mike, apparently toward the door. The Priest himself wasn't nearly as effusive.

A few minutes later Operations buzzed. The Priest and his get-away driver were leaving the garage. The radio cars had been alerted. It would be a matter of minutes now until the two were picked up.

Greg got on the direct connection that Termie had lined up with the Tech Room. George Benson repeated word for word Hoagy's talk with Harry Malone that was in progress over Old 66.

"We're all set, Blitz," Hoagy said.

"Good."

"I'll cable you soon's I get there, and again when I set the deal."

"Good," Malone repeated. . . .

The second phase of Operation Malmo now began, and time became a physical weight on him, his watch hands a quarry to keep in sight at every turn.

He stayed at the playback with Termie. They could hear Hoagy moving about, each step one of haste.

It was eleven forty-two when Operations buzzed them. "The taxi just pulled up. The driver's gone inside."

The driver was a police officer. Surveillance had learned the taxi company Hoagy patronized.

"I'm on my way," Greg said, getting to his feet. His legs were stumps as he moved them uncertainly. "Keep in touch with Tech. We may need you."

"I'll pull the bug first," Termie said. "Take me about ten minutes." Over the playback they heard the driver at Hoagy's door, helping with the bags. Hoagy said urgently, "I've got to catch a midnight plane."

"We'll make it, sir," the driver assured him.

Greg left, taking the corridor in long strides. As he stepped into the street he surprised a couple kissing good night, said, "Sorry," and walked to the curb in time to see Hoagy climbing into the cab. As the taxi eased into the street, Greg's car pulled up to the curb.

They followed far behind, sometimes losing the cab. The "cabbie" himself kept them posted. Under the pretext of reporting to his office, he let them know there had been no change in plans. "Cab 23," he said, "en route to airport."

Other radio cars followed on parallel streets, not unmindful that Hoagy might shift his plans suddenly, and very mindful they were convoying $400,000.

At the airport they cruised by Hoagy's taxi, which was parked in a loading zone. Porters hurried ahead of Hoagy as Greg slipped out of the moving car and doubled back on foot. He took up a position on the sidewalk where he could look through the open doors to the ticket counter beyond. Hoagy was weighing in his three suitcases and two traveling bags. He was in his shirt sleeves, a coat over his arm, his tie loosened at the collar. He had a big, good-natured grin on his rugged, outdoor face as he talked with the agent.

Greg felt his insides clench up.

Hoagy handed over some bills, waited impatiently for his change, and headed in the direction of the ramp leading to the plane. Greg cut through the station, jostling people struggling with their baggage or trying to corral children, all irritable under the heat blanket of the night. He walked to the chain-link fence outside where a couple score persons waited to watch the take-off, some possessed with the wonder of it all, the wonder of a boxcar lifting itself in flight. He was only half conscious of them, thinking of other nights at this airport, tailing killers and desperadoes of all kinds to the big air liners, or meeting them and seeking quietly and without violence to arrest them. It was always the same—faces bobbing all about him that weren't faces at all, except for the one he was following or looking for.

That one now was moving across his line of vision sidewise, toward the hostess in her smart blue uniform standing at the top of the mobile stairway, just outside the plane. Two men followed him, hurrying too.

And then the hostess stepped inside and closed the door, the stairway was rolled away, and the purring motors stirred and roared and shook.

The plane taxied to the far end of the field. Greg never took his eyes from it. . . .

The hostess asked Hoagy if she might take his coat, and he said, "Sure, honey." His eyes followed her down the aisle. He turned then to watch the tape of lights and dark bulks of buildings unwinding outside. He tugged restlessly against the safety belt fastened about his thick middle.

Behind him the two men slipped into a comfortable slouch for the long run. One fingered a cigarette while the other picked up a folder from the pocket in front of him.

Neither had his safety belt fastened. The hostess noticed but said nothing.

The two men across the aisle were looking out the window and talking. "I don't see her," said one, and the other replied, "Guess she left. Not much fun waving to a plane."

Up the aisle the hostess said to a woman, "Please fasten your seat belt." She looked up to find Hoagy's eyes on her.

At the far end of the field the plane turned about with elephant-like sureness and rolled to an easy stop, preparatory to zooming down the long runway. An epileptic tremble seized the cabin as the motors spun to the fullness of their power. The roar filled all space, cramming it to the bursting point.

Suddenly Hoagy's wrists were in a vise, the handcuffs snapping. He was screaming, but no one heard. He was lunging, but something grabbed his belly and the pain shot through it, sickening him. He was twisting as a hand roughly explored him, finding the weapon.

And all the time there was the roar. . . .

Most of the people had drifted away from the chain-link fence. Greg leaned against it, lighting a cigarette, feeling the beating a man took on a night like this, and wondering—wondering if the seat belt was fastened securely about Hoagy. That had been Lancaster's idea—to take Hoagy when he was strapped down, when there would be little possibility of a gun battle and hence small chance an officer might be killed or an innocent person struck by a stray bullet.

The motor roar at the far end of the field faded. The plane rolled smoothly back toward the ramp it had left, until it grew into a giant hulk on spindly legs before Greg's eyes. He searched the windows for a signal, but there were only oblongs. The minutes dragged agonizingly—it was twelve-four—as the stairway was pushed back to the door, as the trim figure of an air-line officer bounded up, and the door opened at last, revealing briefly the hostess standing there. The detective then motioned her aside and signaled to Greg.

Greg swung about so abruptly he collided with an elderly woman. He hurried on, hearing her say, "Some people!"

At the airport office a young police officer handed him the phone. "They're waiting," he said.

"Tell McTamish it's okay—we just picked him up," Greg said into the mouthpiece.

He could see McTamish at the microphone, his hat back on his head, his collar loose, a handful of teletypes, reading each one in his staccato style as though the news had only broken, as though each story were world-shaking.

The clock on the wall read twelve-ten. It had been close, with only five minutes to spare.

"We can't thank you enough," he said to the airport manager, who showed his pleasure over having been a part of a police setup. He would have something to tell his golf cronies tomorrow.

The police officer turned up the volume on a blond table radio that matched the desk, and Greg fell wearily into a chair nearby.

This was the pay-off—or it wasn't.

McTamish's voice came over in a fast, hard beat, so unlike the McTamish who covered the crime run. "A mock battle raged tonight in the Rocky Hills, ten miles east of the city, as five thousand men began three nights of maneuvers. Beginning at 11 P.M. a heavy mortar fire was laid down—— Flash—I interrupt. Hoagy Anderson, prominent used-car dealer, was stricken by a heart attack a few minutes ago on the midnight eastbound Associated Airlines plane as it was taking off. Anderson is in a critical state. The plane was delayed fifteen minutes—the first time on record—while airline attendants recovered Anderson's luggage from the baggage compartment. Now back to the maneuvers . . ."

"Well, that's that," Greg said, pushing himself up. "We'll see."

He drummed on the desk. Every night—almost—for years Harry Malone had listened to McTamish.

"If he didn't tonight," Greg said to the officer as they left, "I've got another move—but it would be better if he heard it from McTamish."

The plane was taxiing away for the second time as they came out of the building. They walked toward the police car, parked near the mobile stairway.

Hoagy recognized him. He sat handcuffed in the back seat, a bull look on his face. "Lieutenant," he called, "I've got a right to know what's going on here—what's the charge?"

"They'll tell you at headquarters," Greg answered.

"I want an attorney——"

"You can call one as soon as you get there."

"I want to talk to you—by yourself."

"Go ahead—say whatever you want."

Hoagy leaned over and whispered, "I'll make you a deal. I've got a new Cad. Only two hundred miles on it . . ."

"Thanks, I don't make deals."

"What do you mean? Everybody makes deals. What do you want?"

The crowd had met its friends or seen them off and had streamed away. In the airport station only the loud-speaker clearing its throat occasionally came over.

It was twelve twenty-three when he sat in the pay phone booth, dropped in his dime, and dialed the Tech. He found himself possessed of a consuming fear that the third phase might never come off.

George Benson was sitting by the phone. "Anything?" Greg asked.

162

"Nothing," George said. Greg gave him the booth's phone number and afterward walked to the magazine stand and stood looking over the bulldog editions of the morning papers, lost so in thought that the big headlines blurred.

The phone rang in the booth. The second he heard the buoyancy in George's voice, he knew. Malone was calling the principal hospitals of the city.

He strolled outside then, his heart hammering. Malone would tire soon. He would realize the city had hundreds of hospitals, all-night clinics, emergency stations, where a stricken man might be taken. He would know he couldn't cover them all.

He flipped the cigarette into the night as again the phone rang. "He's going over to Marsh's," George reported. "Here's what he said. 'Marsh, I'm coming over.' Nothing more. He hung up before she could answer."

"Tell Termie I'll meet him at the O.W."

He felt the slight breeze on his flushed cheeks as the car sped down dark, quiet back streets. "The heat's broken," he said, to be saying something. He was thinking of all the eyes watching Malone and the ears listening to him, of Old 66, the officers tailing him now, the "window" at Marsh's apartment, the bug behind the baseboard, and the stake-out at the baggage room back at the airport.

"Yeah, but it's going to be a scorcher tomorrow," the young officer commented.

Termie was ahead of him at the Malmo apartment, standing alongside the cameraman by the window. Termie motioned to him, saying nothing, as though he might interrupt the scene that was being played before them.

Marsh was in mussed pajamas, but her hair was combed and her face made up. She was standing stiffly near a lamp whose glow grooved the hard lines in her face. Malone was standing, too, several feet away, tentatively exploring the possibility of moving closer to her. As usual, he was well groomed.

"I appreciate your feeling, Marsh, but——"

"Why don't you send your mother?" she flared. "She's had more experience."

"Please, Marsh, don't. I've been troubled about the other night. After all these years we mustn't let petty things——"

"That woman wasn't anything petty."

"I know, Marsh, I know. God, you're so beautiful. I want it to continue like it has been."

"The only time you ever make love is when you want me to run one of your crummy errands."

He made no answer. Her face softened as she curled up in a chair. "I'm sorry—about the cigarette."

He glanced at his watch. "We haven't much time——"

"What about that woman? How many times——"

"Never, Marsh, I saw her only that once. On my word. Now—they're not careful about luggage at airports. Almost anybody can pick up anyone's. Tell them you're his sister. If there should be any hesitancy, a five-dollar bill should remove it."

"Do I get the Cad?"

"Tomorrow, Marsh. I could wait here for you. You could take a taxi there and back."

"Why don't you go?"

"They would ask more questions of a man—but a beautiful woman . . ."

She stalled, lighting a cigarette. "I—I don't know. I'm afraid, Blitz."

"Could Hoagy have gotten on that plane if anybody had——"

"I guess not." She sat with her eyes on the floor. "I'll get dressed," she said. "Get me a taxi, will you?"

As she was leaving the room, he called to her. "Marsh." She turned. "It's like it always has been?"

She nodded. "I'll get dressed."

His face had the old impassive look as he passed the "window," going to the secretary. As he pulled the phone toward him, he raised his voice slightly to call back to her. "I don't think you have any idea how upset I am. It's been nineteen years—nineteen years —Hoagy and I have been together."

kept the phone line open to Lancaster's office and followed Marsh as the radio reports were relayed. She was nearing the airport, she had left the taxi at the passenger loading zone, she was inquiring at the luggage room. The attendant was hesitant, as he had been told to be, so that her suspicions would not be aroused. A porter was carrying the five bags to the taxi and the driver was piling them in the back seat. The taxi was making a U turn, and finally it was nearing the apartment building. . . .

Malone turned the pages quietly. Once he held his wrist watch close to the lamp and then settled back.

He recognized her soft steps in the corridor. Folding the paper neatly, he placed it on a table and went to the door. He opened it as she was putting the key in the lock.

The taxi driver followed her in with three of the bags. "Over here, please," she said. She returned the key to her purse as he set them along the wall.

"I'll get the other two, ma'am," he said.

He left the door slightly ajar. "You made a quick trip," Malone said.

"I could've picked up all the bags in the place."

He pushed one of the bags with his foot to line it up with the others. "I can't understand Hoagy running about with such cheap luggage."

"Can't you?" The sarcasm was faint but telling as Malone glanced her way. He took her hand tentatively and gave it a hard squeeze. She only smiled—the smile of a woman who has won a minor triumph.

When the driver brought the other bags, Malone handed him a bill which pleased him. "Thank you, sir, thanks very much."

As the door closed, Malone ran his hands swiftly over the bags, finding each locked. "I need a bobby pin and a knife." She brought them and he skillfully sprang one lock.

"I thought you would have forgotten how by now," she said, and he chuckled low.

He had the bag open, his fingers gently exploring the sides. He made a short incision into the lining and pulled out a thin sheaf of bills spread flat. . . .

In the Malmo apartment the only sound was the murmur of film flowing over the sprockets. Greg watched from the "window," his fingers working as each last step in the drama unfolded before his eyes. Termie turned away, bored. With him it was one more job; the fun was in planting the talking bug, not particularly in what the bug said.

As Malone made the incision in the lining, Greg signaled the cameraman, who turned the turret head, swinging the telescopic lens into place. He said into the phone, "I'm picking them up."

He covered the room in long strides. In the corridor he motioned to the detectives waiting in the foyer, and they met him at the door. Slipping a passkey into the lock so quietly there wasn't a click, he pushed the door open in one quick movement and stepped inside, a .38 in hand.

Malone and Marsh swung about, stunned. Marsh saw the gun and screamed.

"We're police officers," Greg said, moving swiftly into the room, the detectives close behind him. "You're both under arrest."

"Marsh!" Malone cried.

"I didn't, Blitz," she screamed. "I didn't. I swear I didn't."

"Shut up," he said.

"Don't move," Greg ordered. "Stand where you are."

Greg held the gun on them while a detective said to Malone, "Turn around. Stand facing the wall." He patted him quickly. "Clean," he said to Greg. Another detective, in violation of rules, ran his hands over Marsh, remembering more than one automatic hidden in a brassière. He was rough and Greg said, "Take it easy, Steve."

Malone stood rigid, his lips pursed, his eyes staying with Greg. "I want to call my attorney."

"At headquarters," Greg told him.

"I'm Harry J. Malone," he continued. "I'm a broker—with offices on The Row. I have identification in my wallet—if I might get it."

"I know you, Mr. Malone."

Marsh, who had been crying softly, broke away and threw her arms about Malone, sobbing. "Oh, Blitz," she cried. "I love you so."

He stood immobile. "I told you to keep quiet, Marsh."

Greg took her by the shoulder. "Miss Marshall, please," he said. She whirled on him, striking him across the face with a hard, stinging blow and then hammering him with her fists. He fell back in surprise, then grabbed her wrists. Detectives seized her by each arm and she went limp, sobbing.

"Officer," Malone said, "I want to make a statement. I was merely calling on this young woman here whose name is Ellen Marshall. I have no knowledge of anything in which she may have been engaged or any crime she may have perpetrated. I am sure you understand my situation. At my age I know I shouldn't have taken up with just anything—but it happens. . . ."

The room had the strange quiet of a sharp, sudden pause.

CHAPTER 33

Cokie pressed the light switch the next evening before stepping into the living room. This was the hardest part, returning home alone to the dark rooms. Sometimes, after finishing at the restaurant, she would walk leisurely through the campus, purposely stalling, so that the policewoman who came each night at eight would arrive ahead of her. Because even though the woman had little to say, still her steps and the brush of her movements were comforting.

The old clock chimed, its hands at a quarter to eight, its notes high and cheerful. She took the loaf of bread and the eggs to the kitchen, where she left them on the drainboard, and then recrossed the living room to the bedroom. After washing up, she changed into a fresh cotton print dress. She was combing her hair when she heard the knock. Her hand stopped in mid-air as she listened, thinking she might be mistaken. She saw herself in the mirror, saw the unexpected fear in her eyes. Everything, even the simplest noise, startled her now without reason. She was frightened by fright itself. It was something growing a little inside her each day, a black pregnancy stirring about.

The knock was repeated. She asked who it was before she opened the door. She heard a low animal rumble that was Panther's idea of a panther noise. Laughing, she swung the door wide open. His leathery face had a slight smile that crinkled the corners of his eyes.

"Golly, I'm glad to see you," she said, offering her hand. He gave it a hard, friendly squeeze and held it a second. He said he couldn't stay; he had dropped by to see if she and Mick would like to attend the matches.

"I'm taking on a tough customer tonight," he added. "The Bomber from Madrid."

"Mick's working, Panther," she explained. "He's got a job as night watchman at the old Derrick tire plant."

"Well, good for Mick."

She smiled, her heart warm. The Panther would like anyone she went with. He was that way, bless him.

"How about you coming with me?"

She hesitated. "I've got studies . . ."

"You're my good-luck charm, Cokie. I always win when you're there." He laughed. "I'll buy you an ice cream soda when it's over. You know the Panther—a big spender."

Something held her back a moment, nudged her and reminded her. Something she didn't want to think of, and so she shook it off. She cast about for pencil and paper. "I'll leave my roomie a note," she said.

"Is that woman cop still around?"

She stopped dead still, looked at him, and then smiled. "You're not supposed to know."

"I can tell 'em even when they're in skirts," he said. "Forget her. You got the old Panther to look after you."

But she scribbled a note anyway.

Downstairs he held the car door open for her and then took the side streets that were fast turning murky. He talked about the time he had wrestled a kangaroo in Australia and another time a bear in Alaska. "I don't know who was the most scared," he said, "the bear or me."

As he was showing her to her seat, people called out, "Hiya, Panther." He left her alone then for his dressing room.

The preliminary matches proved tedious, but the crowd had spent its money and felt obligated to work itself into a yelling frenzy. By the time of the main event the excitement engendered was a pulsing, living thing that rippled across the rows of packed, steaming humanity.

Panther came swaggering down the far aisle in a panther robe, and a thunderous roar went up. He waved like a lord to the peasants and they jeered and screamed. The Bomber went almost unnoticed.

The official introduced them. Their faces already were glistening with beady sweat in the hot, intense glare. The referee started to open the Panther's robe. Panther shoved him away. He shouted, "Get your dirty hands off me, you scum. I'll open my own robe." The crowd went mad.

The Bomber offered his hand, but Panther turned away abruptly without taking it. The bell sounded and Panther let out a jungle roar that the mob took up.

The smoke hung in layers, stinging her eyes. All about her people were shouting. The man in front of her was standing, shaking his fist and screaming. She could hear the television announcer reporting, ". . . a nice takedown with an arm lock by the Panther . . . the Bomber on his shoulders for a one and a two . . . the Bomber corkscrews out of it . . . they break . . ."

When the man in front of her sat down, the Panther was standing perfectly still, crouched a little, his big hammy hands outstretched, waiting. His arm muscles bulged, looking as if they could crush the life out of any man.

He changed his tactics then. He rushed the Bomber with a

vicious dropkick. The Bomber hit the mat face down. The Panther dropped all his weight on him and got a wrist lock.

They were near the ropes, and the Panther's face was even with hers. His jaw muscles were set and his lips pulled back as he twisted the Bomber's wrist—twisted it until she thought she would hear the bone snap. His face was contorted in an expression of animal brutality such as she had never seen. But it was his eyes that sent a tremor spreading over her.

Her heart lurched at the touch on her shoulder. The usher said, "A man outside asked me to tell you your boy friend's been hurt."

CHAPTER 34

When Greg walked into Lancaster's office after sleeping fourteen hours straight, Lancaster was at the files, muttering to himself. "I don't see how those girls ever find anything."

He slammed the file drawer shut, said, "Sit down, Evans," and returned to his desk.

"We're in for a fight," he said, putting a match to a stogie, "but we've got the evidence, and that's what counts. Didja see the evening papers?"

"Not yet."

"Malone posted $100,000 bond for each of them—the way you and I'd pull out a ten-dollar bill. They've got Rice, Wearing and Hodner to represent them." He took a couple of quick puffs to get the cigar burning. "Look at these telegrams. Everybody in the nation who's got a kidnaping or extortion thinks we can wind it up for them—and by thunder, we will a lot of them."

He blew smoke out and glanced warily at Greg. "What'd you want to see me about?"

Greg took a deep breath. "I want a transfer," he said, "back to Homicide."

"Why?"

"Because I want to feel like a cop again—not a second-story man. Until the people and the newspapers and the lawmakers and the courts can make up their minds——"

Lancaster hit the desk. "Damn it, Evans, how can you talk like that when you've sat in the Tech Room—and seen what it's done? You couldn't have cracked Malmo without it."

"I know—but it's——"

Lancaster was on his feet, pacing. "I don't know what all this talk's about. The Fourth—the Fifth Amendment. Maybe the guys who wrote them, if they'd lived today, would have written them differently. Had you ever thought about that?"

Greg waited for him to subside. "I know how you feel—because sometimes I feel that way too—but it's just that . . ."

He trailed off, Dr. Buntin's words marching across his mind. ". . . it's a question of a man's basic freedom . . . whether he can sit down in his own home and feel it is his home and nobody can come into it . . ."

"Okay, Evans," Lancaster said, his disappointment showing, "you get the transfer."

He returned to his desk to indicate the talk was over. He couldn't resist a parting shot. "You're too conscientious, Evans—but you can't help it. It's the damn universities."

Greg walked the six blocks to Tech. A Supreme Court justice had once said something about "the sober second thought of the people." That was what would decide it in the years ahead—the sober second thought of the people.

George Benson got to his feet quickly. Several of the bugs were talking. The clock hands were at a quarter to eight.

"I tell you, if you date him he'll read you by Braille . . ."

". . . the butcher charged me sixty-seven cents and the ad said fifty-seven . . ."

". . . she's a sweet little thing, if you like cobras . . ."

". . . they catch the biggest fish in the country down at that barbershop . . ."

It was the old familiar murmur, the drone of bees about a hive, the purring of a cat.

172

He saw Old 66 then. George had strung a ribbon about the ancient playback. Behind it he had tacked up a crude scroll, "Broke Malmo, September 21."

George said, "Maybe we can get a new condenser—get her voice back in shape."

"Nothing on the Logan case?"

"Not a word."

Tech 12 started chattering then. Mrs. Andrews to Mrs. Peet. "You'd never guess what happened. Joan's almost beside herself. She got a doll this morning—almost as big as she is. You know, the kind you wash their hair and has diapers and all. It had a card with it—said it was from a secret admirer. We haven't the slightest idea . . ."

George looked up with the faint tracery of a knowing grin about his mouth. Greg avoided his eyes. "Let me know if anything comes in on the Logan matter," he said, turning toward his office.

He settled down to battle the paper work. He was about half-way through the stack when the switchboard at headquarters transferred an incoming call. He said, "Evans speaking," and a light feminine voice answered. "Hello, Mr. Evans—this is Jane Meredith at the university."

"Oh yes, Dr. Meredith."

"I've just finished with the voice recordings. Any time you're over this way . . ."

He noted it was nine-ten. "It's getting late—but how about now?"

"Good—I think I have something."

He restacked the transcripts, told George where he would be, and hurried down to the car. Within ten minutes he was winding his way along a campus street that had been a cowpath.

She greeted him pleasantly but briefly, eager to get at her subject. He sensed the tingle of excitement in her voice as he sat in a hard straight chair by her desk.

She began, "I know these two men only by the names they used on the tapes—Blitz and Hoagy. So I will call them by those names. As for the 'they' that Hoagy mentioned—I'll call them the third party."

She hesitated. "Before I go on, I should call your attention to one of the oldest concepts in criminal psychology. It's that when someone breaks away from his normal pattern and tries deception he's going to show it in his physical reactions—in little telltale things that fear and anxiety cause."

She took up a paper. "I noted down these nonconformities in Hoagy's behavior pattern. His voice characteristics fluctuated every time he discussed the third party. His word rate would slow down, indicating he was thinking carefully about his speech. He hesitated a brief second each time Blitz asked him about the situation. Both his slow speech and his hesitation are diametrically opposed to his usual method of talking, which is hurried, positive, and direct.

"I want you to listen as Hoagy says the word 'they' when he does not refer to the third party but to other people. This is the norm—the way he usually speaks the word."

They listened to several sentences she had cut out of the conversations and pasted together. Hoagy's voice in the night quiet of the room was like a ghost talking.

"And this is how he says the word 'they' when he does discuss the third party. You will note that he places added stress on the word."

Greg said finally, "It's as though he's afraid of the word."

She nodded, switching off the playback. "Another thing—after playing the conversations a few times I was surprised—and I know you were too—that the third party had told Hoagy so much. He always knew two basic points: (1) the approximate time of each proposed attack, and (2) the approximate means—that is, by accident. Now it just simply doesn't follow that a slayer would confess his entire crime to Hoagy in advance, blueprint every step, complete with details."

She picked up several typed sheets, neatly clipped. "I've tabulated forty-three direct questions Blitz asked Hoagy about the third party. You will note when you read this that Hoagy gave forty-three direct answers to the questions. He even knew the thinking of the third party. Here he said, 'They figure she's too broken up—and doesn't want to show her sister up for what she was.'"

She smiled. "You know that as close as a husband is to his wife, if somebody asked him forty-three questions about her shopping plans he wouldn't know the answers to all forty-three.

"But Hoagy did. This fact—that he knew far more than he would have known even if a slayer had confided in him—plus the fact that his physiologic reactions when discussing the case indicate deception—well . . ."

He shot her a quick glance. She nodded. "Hoagy is your third party. He is 'they.' He used the term 'they' in an obvious attempt to hide some activity of his from Blitz."

"It fits," Greg said to Lancaster. "We've run a surveillance on him for days, tailed more than a hundred and fifty people he talked with, and never found one who might be 'they.' We've had a tap on his phones—and he's never called anyone who could be 'they.'"

Lancaster was in his bathrobe. They were both standing at the far end of Lancaster's living room, talking in low voices.

"Let's go outside," Lancaster suggested. As he held the door for Greg, he asked, "How do you figure it?"

"I think Hoagy got tired of seeing Malone take most of the money. He was getting fifteen per cent of the take when it should have been an even split. It was Malone's niggardliness that set him to thinking. He decided he would pull a job on his own."

Lancaster interrupted. "You mean the $60,000 bank messenger slaying?"

Greg nodded. "He couldn't let Malone know, because Malone wouldn't have stood for it. But he had to have Malone—to get the money out of the country fast. It was possibly Hoagy's one and only job."

They sat in yard chairs in a cool dark patio. The stars were sharp and low. Greg continued, "We know Jan went into a state of shock the Friday the pay messenger was killed. Maybe Hoagy needed a lookout. We know he had played around some with Jan Logan. So maybe he asked her how she'd like to make a few thousand. It was to be a quick, clean job."

A lean, tall woman took shape in the light of the doorway. She said there was a phone call. Lancaster asked her to get the number.

"Go ahead," he said to Greg.

"Jan, of course, may not have had any actual part in the crime. She may have learned about it somehow—maybe even from Hoagy when he was in a confiding mood—and tried to blackmail him. Any way you figure it, he probably panicked."

Greg paused. When Lancaster failed to comment, he went on, "Jan drank too much and might talk. And Jan was scared, too, because she knew the spot she was in. She did what they all do in that situation. She told Hoagy if he was thinking of killing her —well, she had told someone who would stool-pigeon to the police if anything happened to her. Maybe she said she had told Cokie. And he figured someday Cokie would talk, she would be a witness against him, she would send him to the gas chamber."

CHAPTER 35

The usher pointed out the sleek, two-toned car at the curb, and she was running to it, the pounding of her heart shaking her, her thoughts in a wild scramble. She collided with a newspaper boy, upsetting him. She helped him up and frantically started to pick up his papers. The man waiting at the car door shouted to her and tossed the boy a bill.

"What's happened to Mick?" she cried, falling into the seat. He slammed the door shut behind her. He was a mastiff of a man with a bulldog head to match his big frame. He never looked at her. He moved around the front of the car in easy long strides.

"He was hurt in an automobile accident," he said, raising his voice over the noise of the traffic. He gunned the car, and her head snapped back as they shot forward with racing impact.

"Accident?" she exclaimed.

But Mick was working. He was at the Derrick plant.

"He's got a broken leg—maybe internal injuries," the man continued, and her insides gave a wrench.

He was weaving the car recklessly. His eyes switched back and forth in quick snatches of view from the street ahead to the rear-view mirror.

"Where is he?"

"The West End Hospital."

Oh God, please, please, she whispered. And then a faint suspicion slipped upon her, and suddenly it was something burgeoning about her, wrapping itself tightly until she could have screamed.

"How did he know where I was?" she blurted out.

He looked sharply at her. "He knew," he said bluntly.

Mick couldn't have. Mick thought she was home studying.

She squirmed closer to the door. He was watching her out of the edge of his vision. Her moist hands went over the door in frenzied haste. There was no handle, no knob, no way of opening it. The glass was up, in spite of the hotness of the night. She screamed as he braked the car to a stop for a red light. He swung his left fist for the dead center of her face and caught her across the lips. Her head doubled back, hitting the car seat.

"I've got a .45 on you," he said, shoving the gun roughly into her soft side until the pain was excruciating. "If you scream again, I'll let you have it."

The red changed to green and he gunned the car ahead of the traffic. He drove with his left hand, his right punching the weapon into her with the movement of the car. They had left the city behind—she didn't know when—and were in the darkened suburbs. Only the corner street lights and an occasional car streaking toward them cut shafts in the night's blackness.

"Have you ever seen what a .45 does?" he asked. "It'll cut you in two, dump out all your insides."

The detective shadowing her had looked away for only the few seconds it took Panther to win his first fall. When he glanced back, she was gone. He stumbled over a man's shins getting to the aisle and hurried outside, where he learned from the newsboy what had happened.

As he ran back into the arena office to phone Homicide, he swore to himself. It wasn't fair, putting only one man on a tail job.

The sergeant on duty rousted Akers out of bed. Akers began the operation by telephone, and ten minutes later reported in, buttoning his shirt. Greg arrived a minute or two afterward, his throat dry.

By then an all-points bulletin had gone out, carrying Hoagy's description and hers, and that of Hoagy's car. The news—a suspected kidnaping—had been released to the radio stations for their night-owl broadcasts and a special bulletin sent to the disk jockeys.

When Lancaster arrived, his eyes weary with the strain of the night before, Homicide already had enlisted the help of the sheriff's office and the highway patrol. Within minutes they set up blockades across the principal thoroughfares, lighted by flares burning eerily in the night. And soon two sheriff's helicopters churned slowly over the starlit countryside, scanning it.

If he fled the city, they would trap him in time. If he hid out in a dingy room on a dingy back street, they might find her body before they found him.

While Lancaster offered an occasional suggestion, Akers hurriedly set up a detail to handle the man hunt. He chose officers to correlate the work of the police, sheriff, and highway patrol, to sift incoming calls from people who would hear the broadcasts, to prepare the bulletins for radio relay, to chart the radio cars and stand ready to move them quickly on order, to check the equipment—the shotguns, the rifles, the tommies, the tear-gas shells, the spots, the handcuffs, the leg manacles.

Greg asked permission to check out a lead. Taking another detective, he hastened to Hoagy's used-car lot, which was lighted like day. As they crossed the street, Greg saw Hoagy's car—the one described in the all-points bulletin—parked alongside the office.

A heavy-set, burly salesman shook the sleep off as they stepped into the office. He rose groggily. "We're police officers," Greg said, showing his badge. "Which car did Hoagy Anderson take out of here tonight?"

The man came awake. "What didja say?"

"You heard me."

The man squirmed. "I didn't come on until eight."

Greg grabbed him roughly and shoved him. The office shook as he fell against the wall. "I asked you a question," Greg said.

The man swallowed. "You guys come rushing in here—a fellow's half asleep—and push him around. I don't like it."

Greg shook him. "Come on, we're taking you in."

The man sputtered. "It was a 1955 Buick."

"What color—what model?"

"A hard-top, two-tone job, gray top, blue sides. White side-wall tires."

He glanced at his watch every minute or two. Time was hounding him. He took the turnoff from the main highway at a tire-shrieking speed but leveled out at a slow, steady grind along a paved country road.

She had shoved fear as far back as she could. She was determined to keep her head, to wait for her chance. She thought, He'll have to take the gun away to make it look like an accident. When he does, I'll be ready.

The road ran in a straight line through flat, unbroken country. A farmhouse, wrapped in the dark, would loom up occasionally. A dog rushed a fence once with a savage growl. The dry fall smell of fodder and pumpkin time was heavy in the air. She stole a glance at her captor, his face lighted by the upglow of the dashboard. He was watching her as well as the road.

She took a grip on herself. "You think I know something," she whispered. "The police said you did. But I don't—before God, I don't."

"I didn't ask you."

"If you'd only talk to me—about whatever it is."

"Shut up," he said, ramming the gun deeper to remind her. He took another look at his watch.

A moment later she noticed with new alarm that the houses had run out. On his side a high wire-mesh fence—too high for farmers —sped straight and seemingly without end. Once the headlights caught a sign near the road, and the words in huge, bold letters —NO TRESPASSING—U. S. ARMY RESERVATION—stood out for one fleeting second.

Her legs were weak and sore and numb. She wondered if they would hold her up, if they had a chance.

He slowed perceptibly, looking to the left. He found a gap in the fence and swung through it. The wire had been cut and pushed to one side.

He switched off the car lights as he took a bumpy, rutted trail a short distance. The vastness of the land and the stark loneliness stirred up the fear in her.

He stopped on a high spot and turned off the ignition. They were on rolling, hilly country, unlighted as far as she could see, except by a blanket of stars low and bright.

The dull pain in her side eased as he took the gun away. He turned toward her then, his weight crushing her, his tobacco smell on her, his body pinning her arms down. He was saying, "Let's see if you're any better than your sister." His lips ground against hers as he forced her head back to the breaking point. She was struggling fiercely, lurching her body futilely against his. His big hands were on her flesh, grabbing hunks of it and mashing and mauling it until the pain shot in a scream to her throat where it was bottled up.

He lifted his weight at last and sat back. He was breathing laboriously and his intent eyes were fixed strangely on her. He took a handkerchief to wipe his lips. She waited, like something whipped. He said quietly, "Look, I'm going to give you a break.

180

I don't think you know anything. But I've got to have your promise."

She couldn't speak. She only made a sound.

He walked slowly around the car to her side. Before he opened the door he took a long look about the desolate countryside and referred again to his watch.

She spilled out of the car, pulling her dress into place about her shoulders. He grabbed her wrist in a vise-like hold, his fingernails sinking into her flesh, breaking it.

"You follow this trail," he said. "You see that village down there?"

She wiped her eyes with her free hand and thought she saw the dark forms of buildings in a valley that was little more than a depression. "You can get a ride back to town from there."

He still held her but had loosened his grip. "I've got your promise?"

She tried desperately, but again only made a sound. He let her go. She backed away, watching him step by step. He returned to the wheel and switched on lights that flooded her, blinded her.

He's going to run me down, like a rabbit.

She broke into wild flight, panic driving her, whipping her to the last breath, the last lunge of strength. She stumbled and sprawled flat and lay a long time in the light, waiting for the car to roar down on her.

She was staggering up when she heard the motor turn and fall into the familiar spin. The lights moved away from her. She watched in utter disbelief and without comprehension as he turned the car about. He drove slowly the way he had come. Once she thought he looked back.

Her feet pulled all reasoning out from under her as they took her pell-mell down the trail. She rounded a corner, and hope bounced inside her as she saw a dark cabin ahead to the right. Running, falling, picking herself up, crying out for help, she reached the door. She pounded on it, still calling out, and pounded in frenzy until at last she knew there was no one inside.

Half sobbing, she stumbled away. The place had a deserted feeling. . . .

Shortly after the description of the 1955 Buick was broadcast, Unit 225 radioed to Communications.

"Two twenty-five reporting," the officer said. "Just before your broadcast came in, we followed car matching description one mile west on Highway 80 as speed suspect, but driver kept within limit. Car turned north on Devon Road."

Communications came alive. Akers, Greg, and other officers crowded into the hot, sticky, sweaty room. Greg pulled down the five-mile-square chart of the area and plunged red markers into the map as Akers said, "We'll set up road blocks at 80 and Devon and at Devon and Wilson."

A Communications officer was talking to the sheriff's office. "It's a county," he said, raising his voice above the growing babble. "May we come in?"

He turned to Akers. "It's cleared," he said.

The teletyper was pounding out, SUSPECT BELIEVED ON DEVON ROAD NORTH OF HIGHWAY 80. ROAD BLOCKS BEING SET UP AT DEVON AND 80, AND DEVON AND WILSON.

The monotonous, flat voice of the mike man was saying, "Units 46 and 278 move to Devon and Wilson. Proceed to set up road block. Suspect believed headed that way from Highway 80. Units 188 and 77 move to Devon and 80. Suspect believed headed north but may double back."

Akers said to the equipment man, "Okay, get rolling," and to Greg, "You take charge at Devon and Wilson. We'll radio you if he doubles back."

As Greg left the room, he heard Akers asking, "Anything from the helicopters?"

Greg took the stairs two at a time to the subterranean garage, where the cars were rolling out smoothly one by one. Two other detectives hurried to join him as Akers began to build up his manpower at the key point of Devon and Wilson.

The hot air stung their faces once they left the frustration of city traffic behind them. . . .

Hoagy cruised slowly along Devon. He would wait for the show.

There was no possible chance she might escape, but if she did, she would come back this way to pick up a ride and he would be waiting.

He was amazed at how easily all the little pieces of the plan had fallen together, once he'd put his mind to it. He'd been crazy up there at the lake, stalking her and then trying to grab her. He could see that now. And later, when she'd come back to town, he couldn't get to her right off, and the Madrid trip had come up, and he'd thought he could forget about her, get to Madrid with all that money, and disappear somewhere in Europe. But she always would have been around, and if they'd caught up with him sometime—well, you never ought to go off and leave any unfinished business. Who would've ever thought that he'd be picked off that plane?

And now an exhilaration he hadn't known in years filled him. It was like the old days with Blitz and Marsh, when danger was something you hunted down and lived with.

He felt again the squirming, lunging body under his, the resisting lips, the tender give of flesh in his hands.

Everything would be all right now. Blitz would take care of the charges pending in the money matter. Blitz was clever that way; he would maneuver for months; he would slip out of it with legal gymnastics. But this—this business of Jan's sister—she would have sent him to the gas chamber, and there would have been no escaping it. Blitz would have deserted him. Blitz would have figured it as a double cross.

He had been foolish; he knew that now. He guessed Blitz was right. He plunged into things without thinking; he was too much a man of action, but damn, that's how he liked to live.

Jan had been sitting at the bar, swinging her long legs. He figured she would be interested for five thousand—and for five thousand she would feel obligated to him. She had hesitated, but after the third drink had warmed her insides she had asked when.

He couldn't have foreseen what would happen. Nobody could. Who would have expected that doddering old codger to pull a gun? Not that he minded killing him, but Jan had. She minded a lot. And when that little broad was drunk she talked too much, and when she sobered up she would blackmail him for every cent and then turn stoolie. He remembered her saying, "If you're thinking what I'm thinking, don't—because I've told my sister, and if anything happens to me the police will know."

His mind flea-hopped. He wouldn't have known where Cokie had gone on her vacation if it hadn't been for Jan. She had dropped it in an idle remark. He was smart that way. He never missed the casual talk.

He held his watch up. Only three minutes now. It was an inspiration. Nobody would even suspect it hadn't been an accident. They would only wonder how she had gotten there. They might think of him, since he had shaken the two cops tailing him. He'd spotted them a half hour after the lawyer had sprung him. But nobody could prove anything. That was for sure.

At the first sound of the churning overhead he put his head out the window. A helicopter was cruising low. He watched it then through the windshield, hunching down so he could look up. When it pulled ahead of him, he relaxed.

Then he saw the flashlight waving across the dead center of the road. He shoved his foot down on the accelerator, grabbed the steering wheel, and swung about in a U-turn. A siren was in his ear and motorcycles were roaring about him. He drew in his breath sharply as the helicopter sat down almost directly in front of him. He wrestled frantically with the wheel and cleared it by inches, only to crash into a police car that loomed up suddenly from nowhere.

A head looked in on him. "Where's the girl?" it demanded.

He was shaken up but not so he didn't recognize the face. "I remember you," he said. "You're Evans."

"What have you done with the girl?"

Then the sky lighted up and low thunder rolled over the hills. . . .

She settled to a steady walk since the village looked a half mile distant. She thought once of turning back but feared he might be waiting.

Her legs would scarcely support her, and a recurring tremble that was at times spasmatic swept her.

It was a barren land. As far as she could see in the dark, there were no trees and only a few withered shrubs. The trail had been used recently, apparently by trucks, judging from the jumbo tire marks. She was puzzled by the potholes, looking as if they had been blown out of the earth, that became more frequent the farther she went.

She missed the night noises that rise from any land, the occasional murmur of a bird, a rustle in the brush, the music of crickets. This was a silent country she was walking through, her steps in the sandy soil the only noise.

She thought, It is a land afraid, like myself.

The village lay shrouded in blackness as she approached. She looked for a light somewhere, a light behind a window shade, some indication of life, but there was none.

She started down the dirt street, wondering which door to knock on. She looked for signs, but there were none. Something flapped in the breeze and the odd noise startled her.

She stopped then, transfixed, a new fright sweeping her. In that instant she knew no one had ever lived here, no one ever would. It was like a movie set. The false fronts were black oblongs and rectangles without depth against the starry sky.

She felt the cataclysmic shock of the earth as it blew up behind her with a blinding white flash and a deafening explosive roar. The village before her jumped and swayed. Across the horizon other white flashes pierced the blackness. And then ahead of her a hundred yards the ground opened up in another blinding explosion and spewed out in a rain of hurtling rocks and boulders, knocking her off her feet.

She had a faint, faraway awareness she was hurt and bleeding. . . .

Greg asked an officer, "What's that?"

"Army maneuvers. The papers have been full of it. They were to start moving at eleven."

Greg swung back to Hoagy. "Is she out there?"

Hoagy laughed. "I'm by myself taking a little ride in the country to cool off . . ." He trailed off weakly as Greg took a step toward him.

"Take him in," Greg ordered. He walked swiftly to a radio car and picked up the phone. "Evans to Akers. Request ask Hanover army post to hold fire. Kidnap victim believed under fire. Repeat." He handed the phone to the officer at the wheel. "Repeat it," he instructed.

The sheriff's deputy in charge was dispatching a car. "It's fifteen miles by road to the firing area," he said, "but a car might reach it before the phone message clears down from the commanding officer."

"May I borrow your helicopter?" Greg asked.

"Sure—but don't get it shot down unless you want to pay for it."

He climbed in beside the pilot, a Korean war veteran he knew slightly. The ship quivered and groaned as it rose straight up.

"Into that flak?" the pilot asked.

"What about it?" Greg countered.

"Okay by me—if the kid's there."

They skimmed along a little above tree height, following the road. To their right they saw the lightning flashes as the battle stations laid down a heavy mortar fire over a wide area, lobbing the shells far across the rough terrain. One second the hills would light up like cardboard cutouts against the sky, and then as quickly vanish in the blackness. "God," said the pilot, "I feel like I was back—and want to get the hell out."

They came to the gap in the fence. They turned inland, striking across country toward where the first mortar shells were blowing up, until they came to the mock village. "Smells like it," the pilot said. "Smells of death."

They climbed well above the fire. As they cruised along at lobster speed, Greg dropped parachute flares, leaving the countryside behind in a yellowish, nightmarish glow, punctuated by white lightning. He scanned the ground intently, hoping, praying, fearing nothing living could survive. He saw her then. She was waving frantically, a lone figure on the barren land, running after them. Then a mortar shell exploded directly under them and the ship rocked in the backwash of the shock waves. When the smoke cleared, and the dust, he couldn't find her.

The pilot circled patiently, still above the range of fire. Now and then the ground beneath them exploded in violent upheaval, and a second later a tremble would run through the ship.

Greg found the ladder, which last had been used to rescue flood victims, and fed it out carefully, until it was dangling in air, far above the ground. They cruised the same route again, and when they were at the spot where they had seen her before, the pilot held the 'copter steady. It was a peculiar sensation, like sitting in a rocking chair suspended in space. The shell fire was falling heavier, until it seemed the very land itself was in explosion.

And then he saw her.

"How about it?" he asked the pilot.

In answer, the craft dropped slowly until it was under the blanket of fire. "That's it," Greg said when the ladder was skimming the ground. They stopped over her.

"God," said the pilot as a shell cut the air so close they could hear the swish.

She got her feet anchored on the last rung and her fingers clutched about another. Greg said, "Okay, take it up." He scarcely breathed as he watched her. The helicopter rose gently, but the ladder was swaying. Her clothes were half torn from her, and her face, when she looked up, was contorted in pain. She forced a foot up to the next rung and hesitated. Again a shell blasted the ground, and the craft lurched. Her foot slipped.

She clung precariously to the ladder. Greg called to her, but the wind whipped his words away. And then the land went quiet and dark.

"Take it down," Greg shouted. As the ladder touched the ground and raked it, she fell. Before the craft had stopped rolling, Greg was running back toward her. He saw the bloody, torn shoulder.

He picked her up and handed her through the door to the pilot.

He stood a second, looking out over the silent land that had been in such upheaval moments before. He took a deep breath, then climbed in.

He doctored her the best he could, letting her sob, not knowing what to say. Finally she murmured, "Mick—I want Mick. He's all right, isn't he?"

"He's plenty all right," Greg answered. "I'm glad we were wrong about him. And Panther too."

She fell silent.

A good feeling ran through him, and at long last he let weariness overtake him. He dreamed it was Cyn beside him and Mr. Adam watched them, muttering low.